Shame In Me

REVISED

By Jo Ann Felton Carter

Other books to enjoy by
Jo Ann:

ABANDONED NO MORE

SECRETS & THEIR LIES

WHO ME 4GIVE?

VIOLATED

Published by Prospering Soul Publishing 14455
Gannet Streetl Corona, CA 92880
www.aprosperingsoul.com

Prospering Soul Publishing is totally committed to
publishing works that edify and exhort enabling the
reader to prosper in their soul as stated in III John 2.

Published in the United States of America ISBN:
978-0-9892671-6-8 book
978-0-9974419-9-4 ebook
Christian Fiction

SHAME IN ME

Prologue

Let me take a few minutes and explain why I write about issues we have that hinder us from maturing. One day while studying the Word, I stumbled on III John and realized I should focus more on getting my soul to prosper. The only way to do that is to line my life up with the Word. Now that will definitely cause maturity and growth.

Let's get an understanding how the soul and the Spirit entered into Adam: (Genesis 2:7) "***And the Lord God formed man of the dust of the ground, and breathed into his nostrils the breath of life; and man became a living being.***" Here we see the image of God enters Adam the same time Adam's soul, (will, personality, emotions, thinking patterns) does. King James version says, "***...and man became a Living soul.***"

Adam ate the fruit of the knowledge of good and evil and his Spirit man died, (the image of God). Genesis 2:17 (**"but of the tree of the knowledge of good and evil you shall not eat, for in the day that you eat of it you shall surely die."**) Now, to become "whole" again we must, be 'Born again' of the

Spirit. Adam, no longer housing the live Spirit of God caused everyone born after himself to be born of our sinful or soulish nature. We are totally governed by our five senses; what we see, smell, taste, touch and hear.

Mary conceived Jesus after she became overshadowed by Holy Spirit. Making Jesus Christ born without sin and The Lamb without spot or blemish. Jesus dying on the cross makes us able to become born again of the spirit. Being born again introduces us to the spiritual realm, now we are able to become complete and whole again.   Balancing our lives with Holy Spirit and our soul now begins.

We really are aligning who we are with who our Father intends us to become. Having walked totally dependent on our intellect causes a lot of mishaps and healing now becomes very necessary.

Without Holy Spirit active in us, we are not completely whole. That's why we feel as though something is missing, we just can't seem to put our finger on what it is. We travel places, buy things, consume things trying to fill the void in us. What's missing is a relationship with the Spirit of The Most High

God, His image. So, now we understand why we are not totally whole until His spirit functions in us again.

III John 2 & 3, states, "**Beloved, I pray that you may prosper in all things and be in health, just as your soul prospers. For I rejoiced greatly when brethren came and testified of the truth that is in you, just as you walk in the truth.**" The words, "**as your soul prospers**," imply an ongoing work in us and life itself produces situations that will supply enough material for us to work on.

Because the root of our understanding stems from our childhood and, our "method of reasoning" is also developed in our youth. I use childhood memories as the focal point of gaining understanding. When we become "born again." The "mind of Christ," must now become the root of our understanding. Applying the Word must become our method of reasoning.

So I encourage you to spend time studying the Word and time in His presence daily if possible so your relationship with Christ; The Word, deepens and your understanding becomes enlightened.

Trust Holy Spirit and give Him permission to counsel you; get to know Him. He knows your heart and intent even when you don't. Isaiah 9:6 tells us, "***For unto us a child is born, ... And His name will be called Wonderful, Counselor, Mighty God...***" Jesus is THE COUNSELOR!

Create an atmosphere of worship and wait for Him to guide you into your, "session" with Him. Be confident Holy Spirit will not condemn you. He has a way of showing you yourself and not condemn you. Study the Word daily so when He speaks, you will know it is Him, He will confirm His Word.

Fiction is my choice of writing because it is so much easier to see our own faults in others, not ourselves. In 2 Samuel 12:1-9 Nathan tells David a parable of a rich man taking a poor man's only lamb to serve as a meal for his guest. David was furious and stated the rich man should repay four lambs to the poor man and be put to death. Nathan told David ***he*** was the man in the parable; only then was David able to see himself.

This topic, 'SHAME' came about as a result of my living with someone deeply affected by shame.

I must remind you, all stories are fictitious; they are not actual events that happened to neither me nor anyone I know. Enjoy!

CHAPTER ONE

No Way Is This Happening
A Saturday to remember!

This is not happening to me! I must be dreaming, no, I am dreaming! Maybe if I close my eyes I'll wake up. Still here! I have to be dreaming; no way is this really happening to me! I know I am not in jail. I must be having one of those dreams that seem real. I could not possibly be in jail for real! Oh Lord, I *am* in jail! How did I get here? I don't believe this! How did I end up here, in jail? Me! In jail!
Loud speaker:

"....MONTGOMERY, MARVA"

Policeman walks to the front of the room and states, "all of you get one phone call, the line forms there."

Oh, that's me. Why is this guard pulling my arm so hard, doesn't he know his own strength! What inhumane treatment. Oh Lord, you have got to get me out of here! I don't belong here. Jesus, help me, please.

I want to cry but I'm afraid if I do, the others being arrested will think I'm weak and I don't want anyone to pick on me. I'd better keep a straight face so no one will know how scared I am. My goodness, how in the world did I end up here, me, in here? In the name of Jesus; I decree protection over me while I'm in this place. Cover me with Your Blood, I promise, Lord; if you get me out of here, I'll never come back.

I know I should have never written those checks, but I've written checks before... What's wrong with me? Standing here decreeing and justifying my wrong in the same breath! What have I become? I know writing bad checks is wrong. How did I become this? What happened to me? Lord I know better, please, I really need you...

This is so strange. Now I can't stop the tears, and I don't care who sees me. Lord, I really need to feel your presence now. Help me Jesus. I want to know what caused me to become this person that justifies writing bad checks. I need to know the precise cause of what made me think, no wait, what made me *not* think about writing a check that wasn't any good.

I have to know what type mindset I captured; so I can avoid it and never allow that type of thinking to overcome me again because I never ever want to come back to this place. This is unbelievable! *me* in jail!

Who can I call? Mom will be worried, uh, not to mention enormously disappointed in me. And I don't want any of my siblings to know I've been writing bad checks. They all look up to me. Out of the seven of us, I am the only grown child with no kids out of wedlock. They all brag on me because I own a real nice Condo, a CLS 550 Mercedes Benz and, I have been Senior Executive Accountant for Beckman and Jacobs Law Firm for over two years.

Beckman and Jacobs is the most prestigious law firm, not just here in Mableton but in the whole state of Georgia. I really do have it going on and look at what I did; landed myself right here in jail. I'll just skip my phone call for now I am too embarrassed to call anyone.

Whew! Finally I'm in a cell and it's empty. Thank you Lord I know you orchestrated me being alone in here because I have never, in all my twenty-four years of life, ever have been this scared. Growing up in the low income areas of Chicago, I know the definition of scared. While in line getting my "wrinkled jail issue" orange jump suit, I heard some women talking about a church service in the chapel tonight that starts at six thirty and I'm definitely going to attend.

As I was being escorted to my cell, I asked the female guard if it would be alright for me to attend the services this evening. She told me Administration encourages the inmates to attend and she also informed me the preacher speaking tonight is excellent at breaking down the Word. If I wanted to attend, she would have to come and escort me. I told her I would appreciate it.

I really want to check the service out. I haven't been to church in so long. I'm ashamed to admit it, but there was a time when I had a really close relationship with the Lord. Uh, I wonder exactly when did my love for Him diminish. When did I withdraw from His presence? How did I get to this place of not even knowing I wasn't in fellowship with the Lord anymore? When did I stop putting God first in my life? I have a lot of self examining to do...

Lord, I know I have a lot of nerve asking you to

deliver me out of here but I'm asking and while I have your attention; I also want to know where I slipped away from you and what caused me to slip away so I can make sure it never ever happens again! I must find out at what point in my life I took on the mindset that writing bad checks was no big deal. Holy Spirit, please show me where I went wrong... I repent of my sinful ways, I truly am sorry...

Look at me standing here like I'm just visiting, this is crazy. I might as well sit down and get comfortable; I'll be here until Monday. This is truly a shame; in fact it's a crying shame if I wasn't so stunned, I'd be crying right about now but I have got to figure out what happened to me, what put me in here.

I should be home reading my book, waiting for Mom to call, instead I'm in jail. Huh, what a joke, me Miss Marva in jail on a Saturday night. Little Miss boring not home reading. I live the most boring life of anyone I know. I have had the same routine since I started work over three years ago. You can set your clock to my daily schedule. I always do the same thing at the same time.

Tuesday, Thursday and Saturday mornings I make it to the gym from six to six forty-five a.m.. On my way home from the gym I stop at "Doughnuts & More," a family owned bakery just a block from the gym, and I have breakfast; a blueberry bagel with cream cheese and a hot cup of herbal tea. Monday, Wednesday and Fridays, on my way to work, I stop at "Lil Lucy's Café" and grab a cheese filled croissant and a cup of hot herbal tea for breakfast.

During my morning break at work, I have my lunch and I purposely set my lunch time from four-thirty to five p.m. so I can have my dinner. I have five local delis programmed on speed dial in my office phone this way I have my lunch and dinner delivered to me at the office.

When I arrive home from work I get my mail; pick out my clothes for the next day and I crawl into bed with my book. I talk on the phone with Mom, and my older sisters, Stacey and Janelle every night except every other Friday. That's when I call Mom as I leave my office and talk to her while I drive from work to the "Panache Bar and Grill" located here in Mableton. I've been going there for over a year now. The Panache is where I meet two of my office associates, Kayla Braxton and Lisa Ardmore. Kayla supervises the Personnel Department and Lisa supervises the Court Clerks.

They know who's doing what with whom at work and all of the juicy details of the current shock and awe cases. Kayla and Lisa get to the Panache before I do and the more wine they drink, the more information I get. I just sit, smile and drink my seven up and cranberry juice while my ears get full. Oh my goodness, I wonder what the buzz in the office will sound like about me being in here! I'd like to be a fly on the wall to hear that!

Saturdays after exercising and breakfast, I have "Me Time" then I shop. I have a standing eight thirty am appointment for my hair. I Leave the shop and go to my ten thirty manicure and pedicure. Then I shop for the house. I purchase whatever is needed, towels and sheets those sorts of things. Afterwards

I'm off to the mall or boutique, depending on what I want to get. After that I pick up some groceries for the weekend and head home. Once home, I'm in with a good book while I lie on my chaise and read until late Sunday.

The only time I divert my Saturday routine is if I have to attend a previously planned event, like a play or by invitation only affair. That's my quiet, predictable boring life. How I ended up here, is what I need to figure out. I need to know what would make me write checks I know I shouldn't and think I don't belong in jail. When did I stop having a consciousness of doing right and began entertaining the idea of doing wrong? Now that's what I need to figure out by Monday.

Today began as any other ordinary Saturday for me. Even with my animated imagination; I never would have been able to paint this picture. Me spending the night, or shall I say the weekend here in jail!

After I exercised, I had my bagel and tea, went home showered, dressed and headed to my hair appointment. Last week I finally broke down and let my cosmetologist, Rashida cut my hair. Every since ninth grade I have always flat ironed my hair or wore a French roll. I have been complaining for several months about being bored with my hair and wanting to do something different and Rashida has been trying to convince me to let her cut it for some time.

So I caved in and let Rashida give me the "Atlanta Kandi Cut" as she called it. Today, because my hair is short I didn't use all of my appointment time and as I left the salon I noticed a "Just Opened" sign outside three doors down. It was a new café, "Hanna's Manna" and I decided to check it out. When I say you can get the best three cheese omelet in all of Georgia there, that's putting it lightly; Oh the butter!

After eating my omelet I drove over to my manicure and pedicure, left there and was off to the Galleria Specialty Mall to purchase a new set of throw pillows for my bedroom chaise. Because I read a lot while on my chaise, I replace my pillows every three or four months. However the ones I purchased today were very expensive but on sale so they shouldn't go flat too soon.

I left the mall and drove over to the Neiman and Marcus in the Marketplace on Peachtree Road NE. I must get a gown to wear for Judge Berkshire's retirement party being held two weeks from today, September first. Judge Berkshire is a close friend to one of the board members of my firm and whenever we get a "board member memo" inviting us to any function; it is expected of all management to attend.

I must have tried on every rack gown in the store before the sales clerk informed me of some new Michael Kors after five's that had just arrived. I told her my size and five minutes later, I was modeling his latest designs. The lavender draped cowl neckline sleeveless dress fit me perfect! I know fourteen hundred dollars is a lot for me right now considering I would need another fifteen hundred for shoes and purse, but I told her to ring it up.

I thought 'If the check goes through, it goes through.' I changed back into my clothes and went to the register to pay for my gown... Now why didn't I just pause and consider doing the right thing?

Maybe, just maybe, if I can pinpoint my frame of mind at that exact moment, then I can figure out why I would do such a thing.

I am five feet five and I'm proportioned to my height. I wear a size seven in clothing and shoes. When I tried that gown on, I looked up at myself in the mirror, and wow, that gown fit like it was tailored just for me! I slightly twisted myself around as if I were hula hooping, trying to find the price tag to see how much it cost. Hum, I thought as I glanced at it. I looked back up at myself in the mirror and at that moment I thought 'this is the gown, and I deserve it, after all, I do work very hard.' That's when I told the sales clerk I was going to take it.

I knew there was not enough money in my checking account to cover it but I had written checks before at this store and they all went through... Wow, I can't believe I didn't think twice about being dishonest...

What is wrong with me? What's happened to me? I just walked up to the register and pulled out my checkbook and wrote the check like I wasn't doing anything wrong.

The sales clerk went through the processing procedure and the check just would not process. She told me there was a slight problem with her register and for me to go upstairs to the credit offices and they would clear up the matter, it would only take a few moments. I knew the check wouldn't clear, I only had twelve hundred and some change in my checking account.

So I took the escalator down and not up, I headed towards the parking lot thinking, 'that's alright; I get paid Thursday. I'll get a gown next Saturday from "Britney's Boutique" or from "One of A Kind Boutique" over on Austell Road.' Now that the gown situation was settled in my mind, it was grocery shopping time. I started looking through my purse to see if I had put Olivia's grocery list in it. When I stepped off the escalator onto the lower level I was wondering what would be good for dinner.

I heard footsteps behind me and could tell it was more than one person, so I didn't think anything of it. Two plain clothes policemen walked up in sync with me. After three or four steps, one of them asked, "Marva Montgomery?" I closed my purse, stopped, turned toward the man and said, "Yes, I'm Marva Montgomery." The other man stood behind me and grabbed my wrists and slapped a pair of handcuffs on me.

The man standing in front of me said, "Miss Montgomery, you are coming with us." I was baffled. I asked, "Why, who are you, where are you taking me, what's this all about?" They were both silent. The man that stood in front of me started walking and took me by the arm and directed me to the service elevators.

Now as long as I have been shopping at this mall, I never knew those elevators existed until today. I couldn't believe I was being handcuffed like a common criminal. I began shaking my head 'no'; no way is this happening. As we rode the elevator up to the third floor no one uttered a word. All I could think of was they obviously have me mixed up with someone else. When we stepped off the elevator they directed me to a door marked "Security Personnel Only." I thought to myself, 'ok, I didn't steal anything, when they go through my purse they'll see and let me go. Thank you Jesus, this is just a mistake!'

As soon as we walked through the door, we were in what looked like a reception area. There were two long sleek designed candy apple red leather sofas facing each other. To the right of the sofas was a wall that simulated a bank teller's booth with bulletproof glass. Through the bulletproof glass I could see a metal desk with a padded wooden stool parked at it, 'guess the cashier is on break.'

To the right of the booth was a large round smoked black tinted glass table with several high gloss metal and black chairs around it. Directly to the right of the table and chairs was a wood, swinging door.

Out of the swinging door comes two police officers suited in blues, with guns and clubs and they were approaching us. I noticed one of them pull out what looked like a business card from his chest pocket. He looked at the card and began to recite; "You have the right to remain silent...," oh no he isn't. I know he's not reading me my rights! The man never glanced up at me. The other cop walked behind me and waited until the undercover policeman un-cuffed me.

My Juicy Couture Terry Heritage Tote was hanging on my arm when I was cuffed downstairs and considering the weight of the purse and the contents my arms were tingling from the pressure. Off goes the cuffs, but before I could relax my arms, the policeman immediately clamped on a new pair. Oh great, they each have their own personal set of cuffs. Oh no, not another set of cuffs!

That's when I began to panic. I couldn't breathe. I started walking around in a circle, trying to catch my breath. Not helping! I can't breathe! I bent over to try and put my head between my knees but one of the policemen extended his leg and stopped me from moving.

Once I was immobile, the policeman standing in front of me took me by my arm and made me stand straight up. I felt ambushed, and restricted, this is not happening to me! That's when I started crying.

I threw my head back as far as I could and shouted from the depth of my belly, "**What are you arresting me for, I haven't stolen anything?**" Just then the swinging door gave out a squeak.

I turned my head toward the sound to see an elderly lady stepping into the room with us. She looked to be in her late fifties, dressed in a linen and silk blend powder blue Saint John pant suit and she had impeccable blonde highlights in her short cropped hair cut. She was walking towards us with a clip board in her hand and it was full of papers.

I noticed as she reached to grab at her small frameless eyeglasses that were hanging around her neck, how she seemed so deep in thought on what she was reading. As she gently placed the glasses on her nose; never looking up. She stopped and stood next to one of the black chairs by the table and briefly glanced up over her glasses at me.

She began flipping pages and started speaking with a thick deep Georgian accent, as if she were reading a transcript. "Marva Montgomery, you are being charged with 'repeated theft by intent.' You are in possession of store merchandise totaling twelve thousand, seven hundred forty-one dollars and eighty two cents. This merchandise was acquired by you through means of insufficient funds and, is hereby considered stolen property."

Now I was being pulled by my arm out of the same door I came in. Right back to the elevator we had used to come up. I'm thinking, 'so I didn't get away with it. They were keeping a running tab of what I owed.' As the three of us stood waiting for the elevator my mind began rewinding. I saw every item I had written checks for. I saw myself at every register and at home putting each item in my closet. It's hard to believe, me, predictable, boring Miss Marva Montgomery; housing stolen merchandise.

Why didn't I just mail the money to the store for the clothes, or why didn't I respond to the letters the store mailed me? I knew I hadn't paid for those items and now, right this second; I realize... I had no intension of paying for the clothes. I actually thought I had a right to them. My attitude was 'Huh, they gave them to me.' How did I become this person, actually this thief shocked to be hauled off to jail?

When the elevator door opened, a young man suited up in a dark and light brown pinstriped Dolce and Gabbana, was exiting. He had about two inches of platinum spiked hair, and a blue money bag in his hand. The three of us walked onto the elevator and turned around to face the door. I noticed the young man was entering into the door we had just come out of. As we rode the elevator down, reality tried to sink in but my imagination pushed it aside. I just couldn't believe this was happening to me, no, no, no, that's not true, I didn't *want* to believe this was happening to me.

I closed my eyes and imagined myself in my car heading home with a nice aged rib eye steak and a fresh crisp Caesar salad from Mario's Deli, nicely wrapped in Mario's signature bag; lying on the passenger seat of my car. Oh yes, and I am headed home to eat, straighten up the kitchen, wait for Mom to call, rest and read my book.

I was so deep in that thought I even smiled. When I heard the sound of the elevator bell, my imagination slid aside and reality took over. I realized the two policemen in the elevator with me were taking me to Fulton County jail. I can not be going to jail, this is not happening, this is not possible!

The door opened, we were back on the lower level of the parking lot and my two county escorts guided me to a parked police car. I started praying out loud, "Lord, help me, please! Jesus, help me! I'm sorry, Lord, please help me." Now I'm crying and praying, "Father, I repent of my wrong doing, please forgive me Lord. I am so sorry!" By this time we are standing at the rear door of the police car. The policeman who handcuffed me opens the door.

I remember bending over to get in the back seat. Everything that happened after that seems like a foggy motion picture. I really believe I couldn't handle what was happening to me, so I slipped into a place. A place that was safe for me, I just couldn't believe I was actually going through the booking proceedings. I really thought I was watching someone else in my body being booked; this could not possibly be ME!

Now I'm sitting here on this bunk wondering how I came to this. Me, Marva Montgomery, brought up to know better. I definitely need deliverance from whatever caused me to be here. I am going to seek You Lord with my whole heart. I need to know what made me put myself in here, and make sure whatever it is; it is cast completely out of me!

CHAPTER TWO

Brought Up To Know Better
The church in me

As I position myself to lie back on this bunk I'm wondering nervously how much longer I have to wait before service starts. I need to call Mom. I know she's worried by now but I just can't face her yet. Mom calls me Saturday evenings when she thinks I might be home from what she calls "my Saturday shop." She has probably phoned Mr. Williams by now; my only neighbor and I know he's worried also.

Mr. Williams is an elderly wheelchair bound disabled veteran. The weekend I moved into my Condo I sent for Mom and she and Mr. Williams hit it off and before she left they exchanged phone numbers. When I drove her to the airport to catch her flight home, she told me she felt better having a phone number of someone near me just in case something should happen.

Mr. Williams is wise and insightful, especially when it comes to spending and saving money. He had just moved into his Condo the Thursday before I did and later told me it is always less expensive to handle business like that through the week.

He hired a housekeeper, Olivia Rios, to keep his unit clean. Because of my long work hours, I hired Olivia also to clean for me on Tuesdays. She keeps my house spotless, does my laundry including the cleaners, and writes me a grocery list. She does such an incredible job; I'd pay her whatever she would charge because she is worth every penny!

I purchased my Condo brand spanking new six months after I started work essentially for a tax write off. I purposefully picked the end complex because they have two units instead of four. My unit has two thousand five hundred square feet with three bedrooms, two and a half baths, fireplaces in the master bedroom and the family room and it also has a laundry room. The master bedroom has a retreat, a full bath with double sinks, a Jacuzzi tub and two extremely large walk-in closets.

The second full bath is a Jack and Jill, located between the other two bedrooms. The third bath is considered a powder room. It's located near the combination kitchen family room, right next to the laundry room. I use one bedroom as a guest room and the other bedroom is my office slash library.

When I first moved in I would purchase books, read them then file them alphabetically by author in my library. But after the shelves were full, I began going to the local library on Saturdays to check books out to read; it usually takes me four to six weeks at the most to finish a book. My favorite reads are fiction and literature classics.

I'm getting jittery knowing I need to make my phone call, but I just can't talk to Mom yet. I need to do some soul searching first. I have got to know exactly what happened to me so I'll never find myself in here ever again. When I do make my call to Mom I want to be able to say "hey guess what, I'm in jail but;

I know why I'm here and you don't have to worry about me ever coming back!"

The one thing I do realize is; as long as I was attending church, I studied my Word, and was continuously praying and fasting. I never would have considered writing a bad check. I loved the Lord with everything that was in me. We had a strong relationship going on. What happened to me that caused my relationship with the Lord to wax cold? I can't believe I'm thinking about my relationship with the Lord in the past tense; me, miss born in the church.

There was a time I wouldn't let a day pass without spending time with Him or praying in the spirit, how did I forget God, and how did forgetting Him become so easy? Right and wrong was embedded in me, I know better naturally and spiritually, where did I go foul and why didn't I see where I was headed?

Holy Spirit, first of all I repent for all the wrong I've done. I am so sorry and I sincerely ask You to show me how and where I went wrong. Please, I am so sorry for walking away from You. Accept my heart felt apology, please. You promised in 1 John chapter 1 verse 9: *"if we confess our sins, He is faithful and just to forgive us our sins and to cleanse us from all unrighteousness."*

Father, please forgive me... I am not sorry I got caught; I am sorry I wrote those checks and I want to be forgiven and cleansed. I'm confessing my sin, my wrong, please forgive me... I don't have any tissue, oh forget it I'll just use this wrinkled sleeve...

As I close my eyes and cry, I see a crystal clear picture of Mom walking all of us to church, every Sunday, rain or shine. I grew up at Holy Tabernacle Church in Chicago, IL. Because Mom had no means of transportation back then, she made sure wherever we moved was in walking distance to a church, a school and a grocery store. As it turned out Baltimore Street low income apartments was the last move she had to make until she bought her house.

Holy Tabernacle Church was only three blocks from our apartment. Even after Mom would have a baby, she would send all of us to church, making sure someone walked us there and back with Stacey in charge. As long as I can remember, I have always loved to go to church.

My first memory of attending Holy Tabernacle was when I was four years old. We had just moved to Baltimore Street the week before and there were a lot of kids my age living in the apartment building but Mom picked out two of them and sat me down and told me I could only play with Loretta and Britney. She said there would be a class full of children for me to play with when I started school in September.

As we were getting dressed that Sunday morning for church, she told us this church we were attending today has a Children's Church where the children had a class together. I was so happy. Mom said 'class' and I thought it would be like going to school. Monday through Friday I would get up early with Stacey and Janelle and watch them get ready for school and I wanted to go with them so badly. So I thought Children's Church would be like school for me, I was so excited that Sunday morning!

After we were all escorted to a long pew in the sanctuary, I remember slowly looking around noticing everything in the room; the wood floors, the lights hanging from the ceiling and the big wooden pulpit. All of a sudden I heard the most beautiful music playing and when I looked up on the platform I saw a guitar player, a drummer and a piano player. Then there was singing coming from behind me.

I climbed up on the padded wood pew, gripped the top, and rested my chin on the back of my hand watching the choir march towards me and up into the choir stand sounding like angels to my ears. OOH...Seeing those green robes with the gold stoles swaying down the middle isle, and hearing those blended voices, awestruck me.

Later in the service, me Janelle and Stacey went to children's church and I learned the most fascinating story I had ever heard. A man named Noah building an ark and why we have rainbows. I enjoyed church so much and looked forward to going back.

Every day I would ask Stacey, Janelle or Mom, if there was a church service we could go to, in hopes there would be one. When I was around six or seven years old, I remember Janelle being upset one day about having to attend church with me. She and two friends of hers wanted to walk me to church, drop me off and walk to a class mates but because it would be dark when service let out and I couldn't walk home by myself Mom told Janelle to stay at church with me.

Janelle told Mom it was something weird about me wanting to hear Bible stories so much. Mom told

Janelle I had a vivid imagination and I didn't just hear the Bible stories, I had mental pictures of them. Right at that moment, I realized everyone else didn't see the stories in their head like I did. After that I wouldn't tell anyone but Mom about the Bible stories I had learned. I knew she understood me and my imagination.

As soon as I had my tenth birthday I had permission to attend all day time services by myself. All I had to do was find someone to walk with me to the church and back and I was there every time the doors were opened, sitting third row and center. I loved the Bible stories and when I understood Jesus was the Word, I understood I was falling in love with Jesus and wanted to learn everything I could about Him. I stayed in the Bible. I even carried it with me everywhere I went just like it was a novel I was reading.

Pastor Darin Lee and his wife, Sister Alena Lee, were in their forties and they genuinely loved God and lived what they preached. They had four children, two boys Darin Jr. and Phares; two girls, Gloria and Paula. Pastor and Sister Lee always told us, "Living for Christ can be fun as well as rewarding." Each of them encouraged us to have a personal relationship with the Lord.

The congregation in attendance were predominately young adults. Mom had the most children of any of the members. Sister Brenda Rollins held second place with five children. There were a lot of us youngsters and some elderly members, but for the most part, young adults made up the congregation.

Pastor Lee always had some type of activity going on at the church. Hearing the Word inspired me to want to know more and I thought everything I heard was so interesting. With my imagination, I was never bored with church. The first time I felt the presence of the Lord I was twelve. It was the last day of Vacation Bible School and there was a grand finale planned with food and games. I volunteered to help with the preschooler's class.

All of the refreshments were set up outside on the south lawn. Mother Holly told me to go to the kitchen and get more cups, we were about to run out. The church kitchen was located in the basement so I quickly ran through the back door to take the stairs down. As soon as I entered the door, I heard Deacon Miller teaching. His voice was coming from the sanctuary so I decided to take a peek and see who he was teaching.

All of the Deacons were sitting in the choir stand with their Bibles, notepads and pens. Deacon Miller stood in front of them as though he were directing them to sing.

I stood in the doorway listening as he expounded on Matthew 15: 32-37. Deacon Miller instructed them as Deacons, they were to be likeminded and compassionate about the congregation being fed both naturally and spiritually. He went into detail step by step, line upon line explaining how Jesus taught the Disciples how to feed the multitude with seven loaves and the few little fish.

I was so absorbed in the story, I totally forgot about the cups. Mother Holly sent her grand daughter,

Patsy Ann inside to see what was taking me so long. As soon as Patsy Ann hit the back door she said, "I knew it, you're in here listening to some preaching and forgot all about the cups! Little girl, little girl, you are some kinda strange." I quickly turned toward her and noticed she was standing in the door with her hands on her hips shaking her head. After she told me off, she dropped her hands from her hips and walked by me, still shaking her head as she went down the basement stairs mumbling.

I just stood there watching her until she was out of my sight. I hunched my shoulders and thought, 'since she's getting the cups, I'll just sit in the doorway and finish listening to Deacon Miller.'

He explained the importance of their responsibility as Deacons and how their lives should be examples of the Word being alive in them and the importance of the anointing. Then Deacon Miller closed the meeting stressing to them, they should always remember the people were fed because of Jesus compassion for them. After hearing that story I was in awe of the compassion of Jesus. That day I knew Jesus really cares about me and my family. An imprint was made on my heart.

That night I was on my knees praying before getting into bed. I shared the bedroom with Stacey and Janelle. Stacey had her own bed to herself, being the oldest. Janelle and I shared a twin bed, each of us slept at opposite ends. Most nights we read in bed before going to sleep. We may go to sleep at different times, but each of us pray before going to sleep. Janelle had just gotten off her knees and was getting into bed. Stacey was already in her bed going to sleep. I prayed aloud but softly.

I was telling the Lord how much I loved Him and was so thankful He cared about Mom and each one of us. I felt so fortunate Jesus loved me like He loved the people in the story I had learned about today. I began to cry and tell Him I loved Him so much for being such a loving and caring Jesus. I felt a warm peaceful feeling sweep over me. I felt so much love in my heart and a tender sweet presence I couldn't describe. I opened my eyes to see if Jesus Himself was in my room! I couldn't stop telling Him that I loved Him. I just went under the covers and kept repeating, "Jesus I love you so much," over and over. I fell asleep telling Jesus I loved Him.

The next day when Mom came home from work, as she entered the door; I bombarded her excitedly explaining what I had experienced the night before. She told me I was blessed, what I felt was the "presence of the Lord." After we ate dinner, she sat down with me at the kitchen table and said she would help me understand what I had experienced. Ronnie said he was also curious about the presence of the Lord so he came and sat with us. Ronnie is my brother that's almost two years younger than me and frankly I thought he was just being nosey.

Ronnie watches everything I do and tells me constantly what he thinks I'm doing wrong. Because he's a little taller than I am, everyone thinks he's the oldest so I thought he was just being his usual nosey bossy self. Mom said she was so happy to see him have a curiosity for the things of the Lord and she read some scriptures to us and explained each scripture in great detail so we understood what she had read. She even used notebook paper and made drawings on it so we could see what she was saying to us.

When Mom told us about the creation, she painted a picture of the Holy Spirit so beautifully. I was totally blown away! She told us not to be afraid of the presence of the Lord. After she answered all of our questions, she hugged both of us and prayed. A few weeks later I accepted the Lord as my Personal Savior openly at the church alter and signed up to be baptized. I really loved the Lord, and knew He loved me.

After I completed the classes and was baptized, I joined the Junior Choir. I'm not that good at carrying a tune but I enjoyed singing in the choir. The words of the songs we would sing made me feel as though I was singing personally to Jesus. I would close my eyes and it would be me and Him right there and I would tell Him whatever words were in the song as though they were coming straight from my heart.

Very shortly after my fifteenth birthday; after realizing the alto section always had to go over the notes in rehearsal because of me, I left the choir and joined the Junior Ushers.

Sister Emma Hadley, a little bitty woman that had to be no more than five feet tall and wore a size one with a really high pitched voice was over us and I had a blast working with her. Sister Hadley made learning the ushering signals fun. We had quarterly Usher meetings and at every meeting she would say,

"Remember, you are not just serving the people, you are also serving the Lord."

We had to examine a scripture at every meeting and Sister Hadley made sure it expounded on how the Word is constantly being tested in us when we interact with people. She always stressed; "Keep in mind your reaction to how people treat you; is an indication of where your love barometer is. And the only requirement for you to be; and stay an usher is that you grow in godly love."

And oh how I loved wearing my uniform! Our church colors were green and gold so Pastor Lee told Sister Hadley the Junior Ushers could wear white tops and green skirts or pants. I would soak my gloves and blouse with a little bleach in cold water so they would be snow white when I wore them. And I always had something green in my hair that matched my skirt.

Sunday School was *number one* with me. I loved me some Sunday School. That's where I learned so much about the Kingdom of Heaven and how it is here inside the hearts of those that are born again. I would study my Sunday School lesson every night and by Tuesday, I would be finished with the week's lesson. I would go over it again to get more nuggets out of it.

When our Sunday School class studied the Book of Acts, several of us were filled with the Holy Ghost. Because so many of us were filled, Pastor Lee had the Deacons form classes to teach us Who the Holy Ghost or Holy Spirit is and His functions and also the differences in praying and speaking in tongues and prophetic speaking. I really learned a lot and practiced everything I was taught.

During high school I learned about living a balanced life. I discovered I was in this world and had to abide by its set of laws however I was born of the Spirit and could change the very course of nature with my mouth. Because I was very confident in the Word working in my life, I typically stayed to myself. I knew how to be cordial and social and still keep my integrity being spiritual.

Sometimes I would hear a classmate comment about me being too good to associate with them but I never let it bother me. I knew I was born with a purpose and my spirit man rules. I was going to make my carnal thinking and my body be under subjection; that way I would accomplish what it is I am supposed to get done for the kingdom of heaven and I was determined not to let anyone or anything distract me.

I believe my love for the Lord was so strong I never became involved with smoking. It seemed crazy to me to buy tobacco wrapped in paper, light it up, inhale it and blow it out in smoke. That did not make any sense to me, none what so ever! And drinking and drugs, in my neighborhood too many people would act crazy being drunk or high or both and I didn't want anything to alter my mind but the Holy Spirit! Oh no, I was not going to take anything that would make me act crazy, no, not me!

I was curious about sex though. I would listen to Stacey and Janelle talk about what they had heard and I wondered what it may be like. But when I asked Mom, she told me once you become sexually active; it was not easy to stop. I was too scared to try it, I thought I would become a sex junkie and I was not going to be one of those girls the guys called 'easy' and would have sex with anybody in the back seat of cars and in allies. Right then, I made my mind up 'because I love the Lord and want to please Him, I will remain a virgin until I'm married.'

It seems like a lifetime ago I believed in my purpose and thinking about this now, I really miss the closeness I once shared with the Lord. I miss our close relationship and the one heart knitted together friendship I used to have with Him. This is so painful reminiscing on what used to be... Still no tissue... tears are pouring out of me... I must figure out what happened to me so I can go back to my first love...

As I fall to my knees I began saying aloud; "Help me Holy Spirit; help me see where I was when I walked away from You and allow me to see the condition of my heart when I turned away from Your counsel. I want to be restored and have an even deeper relationship than before with You.

Heavenly Father I repent of my wrong doings and I surrender my all to you and your way for my life. Be merciful unto me O God and create in me a clean heart and renew a right spirit within me is my prayer in the name of Jesus. Amen."

I have got to find some tissue.

CHAPTER THREE

Me And My Job
Mirror, mirror of my heart

As I get up from my knees I recall my frame of mind when I left Chicago. It was to come to Atlanta for the sole purpose of attending Spelman College. While earning my degree, I took several business courses. One of my instructors told me: "This class provides proven adequate principals for running a business. However 'observation' is the best method in determining the most appropriate and effective techniques that will best work for the business you choose." So, my plan was to return to Chicago, work for a small accounting firm, get some hands on experience about the do's and don'ts of running a small business then establish my own accounting firm.

That was my plan, however two days before graduation, while packing up my dorm to return to Chicago; I received a certified letter from Beckman and Jacobs Law Firm. They are located in downtown Mableton and are considered the largest and most prestigious law firm in the Atlanta region also; they are referred by other states. They were impressed with my four point seven grade average. My major was accounting with a minor in statistical math.

The letter informed me I was a candidate being considered for the only accountant position available. I was extremely flattered to be considered for the position, so I decided to call and confirm my interview. I interviewed the following Thursday and two weeks later I started working. Only three weeks after graduation and I had a job, and did I praise me some Lord!

The first year I worked as an Accountant I started at the pay rate of eighty thousand per annum. I gave the Lord all His due; first fruits, tithe, offerings and praise because He has been nothing but good too me! I would even sow into various ministries and bless those who were less fortunate. I felt so privileged to be twenty one years old and making that kind of money.

I sent money home to Mom every month until I purchased my Condo. She refused the money and told me to use it to furnish my Condo and for me not to get in debt. I followed her advice and paid cash for everything. After being on the job a month I suggested a software system and because its implementation was a great success I received a hefty six month raise and a bonus at the end of the year.

Exactly one year to the day I was hired, the big bosses were so impressed by the way I made the software training so easy, I was promoted to Senior Executive Accountant. I had nine employees to supervise and my pay tripled plus, they gave me an expense account. This past June, I received another very substantial raise.

Thinking of all this now, I can see it was shortly after my promotion I stopped going to church. I can't believe this. I have been Senior Executive Accountant for a little over two years, and today is the first time I have even thought about why I stopped going to church. This is unbelievable! I can not blame anyone but myself for becoming so 'busy making money' that I almost completely forgot about God. Right now it's so obvious to me it was after my promotion, my Monday through Friday work week turned into twelve hour days; eight-thirty in the morning until eight-thirty at night.

Why did I allow money to separate me from the love I had for the Lord? There was a time in my life nothing would have been able to separate me from the love I had for Him, what happened to me... Well, since I'll be here until Monday I'll lay here and get to the bottom of this. I want to get out of here and never ever never come back!

Now I recall my freshmen year at Spelman. As soon as I moved here I joined Purpose and Destiny Christian Center. My roommate, Roslyn Fitch, was from Cleveland Ohio and her mothers' sister, Ethel and her husband, Greg lived in Bankhead. Aunt Ethel told Roslyn about Purpose and Destiny Christian Center because she and Uncle Greg were members.

After Roslyn visited and told me about what a great time she had at the church, I visited and shortly joined. Uncle Greg would come get Roslyn and I to take us to their house and while Aunt Ethel was getting ready we would eat breakfast. We would all leave from church and go back to the house and have a good Sunday dinner, help clean up the kitchen then head back to the dorm. As long as I fellowshipped at Purpose and Destiny, I was doing all the right things.

Right now I can clearly see my no longer attending church happened gradually. Shortly after I was promoted, the first service I missed was

Wednesday night Bible study. I remember leaving work and going directly to church, but by the time I arrived; the message was over and people were at the alter having prayer. So I decided to purchase that night's CD and while I was standing in line to purchase my CD I thought, 'I'll just purchase all of Wednesday night Bible Study CD's when I attend Sunday services. I get off work too late.'

Yeah, I remember that. Okay now I'm getting somewhere, let me see if I can pinpoint when I consciously decided to stop attending Sunday services.

My alarm clock is always set to go off at five-thirty a.m. seven days a week. However I usually wake up before my alarm goes off. Not long after I stopped attending Wednesday night Bible Study I started turning off my alarm on Saturday evenings, thinking I would wake up in time for Sunday School without the alarm. I remember the first few times not setting the clock, I would wake up at five twenty; go to the restroom and get back into bed and fall right back to sleep. I missed Sunday School but made it to church, and soon after that I started sleeping until nine am.

The first few times I woke up and looked at the clock I thought to myself, 'I must have been extremely tired to sleep that late. I must need the rest.' I hurried getting showered and dressed and drove all crazy trying to get to ten-thirty a.m. service and when I arrived, I felt so rushed it was difficult to get into Praise and Worship. Yeah, yeah, now it's clear to me; I was gradually getting disconnected.

After three or four times rushing to get to service, I decided to just lie in bed on Sunday mornings and study my Sunday School lesson. I stayed home studying until the quarter ended and I didn't have the new book. **Hello!** That's when I stopped setting my clothes out on Saturday evenings, for Sunday. I had no intentions of attending church; none what so ever! ...

Oh Lord, doing this reflection, I can see how it became easier for me not to attend Sunday Services. No longer were my affections set on things above, they were set on my job. Now tears are beginning to drop from my eyes. Oh this is so painful; seeing myself; my selfish self...

I am so sorry Lord. I repent of my selfishness and return to You; my First Love... I really do need some tissue in here, I can not stop crying... this is so painful... oh forget it I'll just cry out to the Lord and let the snot flow... OH GOD HELP ME, PLEASE! ....

I feel so much better allowing my tears to cleanse my soul. I hope they don't think someone is hurting me in here the way I was crying out, emptying out actually. Let me see, where was I ...oh yeah, after missing Sunday Services, I remember mailing my tithe and offerings to the church.

Um, let me see if I can figure out when I stopped sending in my tithes and offerings? Let me think, um, oh no, I don't believe this, it was right after Thanksgiving, yeah I remember. I had done all of my Christmas shopping for my family. It was the first Christmas after my promotion and I was making all that money, oh my goodness, I remember. I went all out buying everyone what they wanted.

I had taken the time to phone each one of my family members to ask what it was they wanted for Christmas and I made myself a list. After each purchase I wrapped and labeled the gift myself and stacked all of the gifts in the family room. Yep, after I had everybody's gift, I loaded up my car and went to a mailing center to ship everything. When I was leaving the mailing center, I noticed a new boutique just three doors down from where I was parked, so I walked over to check it out.

Oh my goodness! I remember as soon as I walked into the boutique, my eyes were drawn to a gorgeous Chanel brown and pale green tweed suit with a crepe waffle patterned shell. I had a pair of Jimmy Choo cognac pumps I just knew would match perfectly. I went into my purse, pulled out my cell phone to pull up my banking app and find out my balance. I had already written my check for my tithes and offering and my balance was a little over fifteen hundred dollars. All those Christmas gifts wiped me out. The suit was twelve hundred seventy five dollars. I would have a little over two hundred dollars to last me two weeks. I spend more than that in a week; with gas, meals, my hair and nails.

I walked around that boutique thinking of how I could take this suit home with me. That's it! Right there was when I decided to no longer give my tithe and offerings to the Lord, the suit went home with me. Wow... this is wrenching my heart, Lord, God! I'm so sorry... I can't stop crying. I have got to get some tissue in here... oh how this hurts remembering that day…

As soon as I walked in the house, I went straight to my shoe closet and pulled out my shoes. I can see myself now almost trembling as I pulled my shoes out of the closet, dropping my purse and keys right there where I stood. My heart was racing I was so excited about the outfit matching my shoes. I yanked the plastic off the newly purchased outfit, oh no, they don't match! The brown on the suit was too dark.

All I could think about was 'what store will I go to next week to find my matching shoes and purse.' I was so excited about my new shopping mission. I never thought twice about robbing God; never gave it a second thought! Lord, I am so sorry, I just tossed our relationship aside like it wasn't precious to me... I can't stop sobbing. Oh Lord please forgive me, I am so sorry...

After that, I never sent any more money to the church. I was so caught up with buying things that I forgot about sowing and giving to the Kingdom of God. I forgot all about the Lord who has been nothing but good too me!

I wasn't aware of my being comfortable with not going to church or no longer honoring the Lord with my finances. Now, I can see how I eased into spending Kingdom money on more stuff. I exchanged my affections for what I considered Holy; for things that never satisfies. When my eyes were diverted off the Lord, they became full of lust for more stuff.

Prayer is the only thing I never stopped doing... Ah, I just realize I have slacked also in my praying. I do all of the talking. I don't enter into worship anymore, nor do I listen for direction. Lord I just complain to You about my problems at work. Oh how I need to find another church. A church that is closer to my job so I can get connected to a local body and be encouraged to seek after the things of the Lord and His presence. Lord I want to reconnect and get an even deeper relationship with You than before. Yes; I want a closer walk with You Lord, an even closer walk than before.

Right now I'm seeing in my mind a tall pile of charcoal burning. The coals are red and blazing hot. Very slowly a coal rolls down the side of the pile, off by itself. I watch the lone coal sit there in one spot and soon, the red color it once emitted, indicating it was on fire, just goes out. Right now I feel like that coal that rolled away. I rolled away from the church, from the presence the hunger and the fire I once had for the Lord and became so self absorbed.

I may have gradually rolled away from You Lord, but I'm desperately going to cling to You now. Lord, I'm so sorry. I repent for putting "things" before You. I want to get back to having a right relationship with You. I want to spend time with You, in your Word and Your Presence, like I did before except now I want to be closer. Forgive me, and restore me; please.

The guard has come to take me to the service. Look at me. My impulse is to look for my purse and keys. Lord did I have it made! Being here is just stupidity on my part considering the freedom I had just this morning. I could go where I wanted, eat whatever I desired, and now I'm being treated like a caged animal. What caused me to become this Marva Montgomery that would write checks knowing I could not make them good, what happened to me?

CHAPTER FOUR

The Root Cause Please
Hello shame

Wow! This preacher, Pastor Houston, is really good. He's breaking down the Word of God so plain. I get it! He's teaching on: "Being responsible for the Word you know." He went to Mark 8:27-33, it states; ***"Now Jesus and His disciples went out to the towns of Caesarea Philippi; and on the road He asked His disciples, saying to them, 'Who do men say that I am?' So they answered, 'John the Baptist; but some say, Elijah; and others, one of the prophets.' He said to them, 'But who do you say that I am?' Peter answered and said to Him, 'You are the Christ'.***

Then He strictly warned them that they should tell no one about Him. And He began to teach them that the Son of Man must suffer many things, and be rejected by the elders and chief priests and scribes, and be killed, and after three days rise again. He spoke this word openly. Then Peter took Him aside and began to rebuke Him. But when He had turned around and looked at His disciples, He rebuked Peter, saying, 'Get behind Me, Satan! For you are not mindful of the things of God, but the things of men.'"

Pastor Houston is teaching us, when we have a relationship with Jesus, we know 'who' He is. Knowing 'who' He is, causes our spirit man to seek after understanding and revelation which; reveals to us His 'times and seasons' for our life. Pastor Houston broke it down to us how just as Jesus had an intimate relationship with the Father and their relationship produced a level of knowing in Jesus of the Father. Jesus knew the times and seasons for His own life, well, our intimate relationship with Holy Spirit will cause us to know and learn to accept the times and seasons for our lives.

Pastor Houston also stressed to us how crucial it is for us to keep our relationship with the Lord pure. He said we must learn how to become sensitive to the times when we are tempted to take Jesus [the Word] aside like Peter did and tell Him what we ought to be doing as we see it. Our being obedient will only lead us to plenty and better.

When he said, and I quote, "Satan or the devil is a thief, and wants to steal the Word from you. The devil wants you to think the things of this world are more important than the Word being produced in you." It was confirmation to me.

Right at that moment I realized the Holy Spirit had allowed me to be arrested so I could take inventory of where I was headed, what I had become. It became crystal clear to me that the Lord loves me so much He is reprimanding me. He is bringing me to a halt so I will stop telling Him what I think is best for me and you know what; I am so thankful He has. I had put making money first place in my heart just so I could obtain more stuff. The will of the Lord and building the kingdom was no longer a concern to me.

As I sit here in this little room, I'm having a visual of myself moving my bedroom dresser to the wall where my headboard was and realize, I had moved my affections from the Lord and His will for my life, to 'acquiring things'. I had moved my affection from being Kingdom minded over to being mindful of getting more earthly possessions; stuff.

Now I see clearly and I'm going to get back in fellowship with the Lord. I'll rededicate myself tonight and get back on the path the Lord has for me. Lord, thank you for being merciful to me and for allowing me another chance to get my heart right with you!

While Pastor Houston was giving an appeal to us that want to get back on the path God has set for us, some alter workers walked up to the front of the room. They all turned to face us and when Pastor Houston completed his appeal, I went up to the front. An alter worker who looked to be well in her sixties walked up to me, smiled and told me not to be afraid while I was here in jail, the Lord was with me. I felt a big weight lift off my heart. I dropped my head and began to weep. I was so sorry for walking away from the Lord. He has been nothing but good too me!

When I stopped weeping, the lady handed me some tissue and stood in front of me. She began praying. "Heavenly Father you see the sincerity in her heart. I speak to her spirit man. Hear, see and obey the Words of the Lord. Holy Spirit; Expose the Root Cause of her being here, in this place as she yields to your control and as You expose, also remove the root. I decree healing and understanding to flow. I bind any hindrances that would try to come against the perfect working of the Holy Spirit, in the name of Jesus I decree these things to be, Amen."

When I opened my eyes she looked directly in them and said, "Don't fear the Holy Spirit; yield and

He will reveal to you the root cause of you being here." When she said that, I thought 'yeah I need to know the root cause of me being here.' Immediately I saw a red neon light flashing the word "SHAME" in all capital letters, "SHAME, SHAME, SHAME, SHAME."

You know like the kind of neon light you see in the windows at some establishments flashing "OPEN." Now let me say I have seen some things in the spirit, but I have never experienced anything like that before, ever. I have always had an imagination but even I would never think neon light?

As I returned to my seat I thought 'come on Marva, neon light!' After I sat down I was puzzled, what does shame have to do with anything?

When I returned to the cell, there was a woman in the bottom bunk. I had left my sheet on the mattress she was laying on. She was curled up in a fetal position, crying like a baby. She never raised her head to see who had just entered the cell. She just kept balling. I saw my sheet on the top mattress, so I just climbed up. Best to take the high road literally, I don't need any drama in here.

Hearing her heartfelt sobbing, I started fighting back my own tears. I covered myself as best I could with the thin sheet issued to me. Finally, I'm settled.

As I lay here, on my back, tears began to stream down my face, trailing directly down into my ears. My heart has agreed to just yield to the cleansing of the tears. I began to softly whisper thanks to the Lord for loving me and forgiving me after

I walked away from Him. Truly, there is no greater love!

I can not sleep. Every time I close my eyes I see that neon light flashing SHAME, over and over again. I'm tossing and turning trying not to see the word. I don't understand what shame has to do with anything. I open my eyes. Now shame is written on the ceiling. I turn over on my side and focus on the wall, there it is. What's going on?

Finally I whisper a prayer. Holy Spirit, give me an understanding of this word shame. This is obviously pertinent to the root cause of me being here. But I can not figure out how, what does it mean? I give You permission to reveal to my inner man the root cause as I yield. Show me what shame has to do with me being in here, in the Name of Jesus I pray, Amen.

Now I'm crying like the woman in the bottom bunk. I close my eyes once again. This time I see myself in my first grade class. My classmates are laughing at my shoes. The pain from their laughter is being felt even now as I remember.

I couldn't wait for Janelle to give those shoes to me. She told me they no longer fit her and when they fit me I could have them. She kept them in our closet and I would try them on every night before getting into bed, in hopes they would fit. I loved those shoes. I thought they were the most beautiful shoes ever.

They were black patent leather and had a small bow on the outside of the shoe, right under the buckle. All the other shoes I had ever seen had a bow on the front of the shoe. These were different; I think that's what made them beautiful to me, being different.

The night before, as every night, I would turn the closet light on and try on the shoes. I slipped my foot into the first shoe and this time, it fit! I was ecstatic. I put the other shoe on and ran to turn on the bedroom light. I had to make sure what Mom had laid out for me to wear tomorrow matches "my" shoes.

Stacey yelled at me to turn off the light, some people had to get some sleep, meaning her. Mom came to the door and asked what the commotion was about. I excitedly told her about my shoes fitting and I wanted to wear them tomorrow to school. Mom went through the closet and laid out the dark grey pleated skirt with the pink and white blouse that had little buttons shaped like bows. I was so happy; my buttons on my blouse match the bows on my shoes! I could hardly sleep I was so excited.

The next morning, I hurried to eat and get dressed. I must have looked in the mirror five times. I just knew my shoes made me look pretty. As Janelle and I walked to school, I thought everyone I came into contact with was admiring my shoes. I must have grinned all the way to school. When I walked into my classroom, still cheesing, Rachael Neal eyed me up and down. When she saw my shoes, I thought to myself, 'she's going to want to try these on!'

My heart fell to my stomach when she began to laugh and point toward my feet. She yelled out, "look at those ugly shoes Marva has on, who wears bows on the outside next to the buckle of the shoe, ugh, and they are so ugly." The whole class burst out with laughter. Even the kids I thought were nice, now they are laughing at me.

I was so mad at Rachael. I just walked to my desk and sat down. No way am I going to cry in front of her. I took out a sheet of paper and pretended to ignore them. Thinking and hoping they would stop laughing, but the room echoed with laughter. The tears were working their way to my eyes but I kept taking long deep breaths to keep them down.

The slower I breathed, the louder the class seemed to get with laughter. Laughter, that's the sound that greeted our teacher, Mrs. Watson. She entered the classroom waving her arms in the air while yelling, "Hey, hey, have you all lost your minds?" I was so glad she came into the room when she did, Rachael would have kept the class going. I could see her in my mind, marching around the room with the whole class marching right behind her, shouting, "Marva has on ugly shoes, nah, nah, nah, nah, nah!"

During recess I stayed inside the classroom. I knew there would be a "Neal Rally" featuring Marvas' ugly shoes. I pictured the whole class lined up behind Rachael, as she cheered, "Who has on the ugliest shoes in the world?" And the rest of the class would yell, "Marva does, Marva does!"

At lunchtime I waited until everyone had left the class, before I did. When I entered the cafeteria I looked towards the dining area to see if it was crowded. I went through the serving line so fast I forgot my milk. Oh well, I'll do without it today. As I entered the dining area of the cafeteria I looked for an empty seat at the back of the room. I didn't want to draw any attention to myself. After I sat down I wanted to take my shoes off, but as I thought about it, that might draw attention to my feet, better keep them on.

That day was the longest day at school ever for me. All I could think about was 'when is school going to be over.' When the bell rang, I ran straight home, now fearing everyone who saw me would laugh at my shoes. I found the key in "The hiding place" and as soon as my feet hit the floor inside the apartment, tears began to run down my face. I ran to the bedroom and kicked off the shoes, now crying aloud. I tucked the shoes in the closet way back against the wall, then I piled all of the shoes in the closet on top of them. 'I don't ever want to see those shoes again.'

When Janelle came home from school, she made a big deal about me coming home all by myself. I forgot to wait for her after school. She was so mad at me for not being at the gate where I usually wait for her and when Mom came home from work, Janelle was still mad. She told Mom to give me a good spanking. Mom asked why Janelle thought I deserved a spanking. Janelle was so mad, she started crying.

She said when I wasn't at the gate she thought something bad happened to me. Mom hugged Janelle and told her she was scared because she loved and cared about her little sister. And that was the reason she was crying. She really didn't want me to get a spanking, she wanted me to be sorry for making her worry.

Mom told me to apologize to Janelle and assure both her and Janelle I will never leave school without her again. Then Mom made Janelle and I meet half way and hug each other. Janelle told me she was sorry for fussing at me and she never wanted me to scare her like that ever again. I told her I would never leave school without her again and started crying because I didn't want anyone to know about what happened to me wearing the shoes. I was so embarrassed.

Mom keeps a big plastic trash bag on a hook inside her closet; she calls it, "The Give Away Bag." Whenever we out-grow something no one else can wear, we are to put it into that bag. When the bag gets full Mom goes through it, makes sure everything is clean and in good condition, then she gives the bag to our church. When I saw her in the kitchen sorting the bag, I saw the shoes among the items. I remember thinking to myself 'good riddance!'

Now, laying here in this jail cell, I'm crying from the memory. I can still feel the pain. I was too angry then to let Rachael Neal see me cry, but now, the tears are pouring out of me like Niagara Falls. My heart is actually hurting. I did not know what it was then, but I know now, it was the first time I felt shame in such a deep magnitude. As I ran home from school that day, I remember making a vow to myself; 'I will never wear anything different ever again!'

Wow, the lady who prayed for me hit the nail on the head, thank you Holy Spirit for revealing the truth and understanding to me.

~~~~~~~~~~

I can't believe I slept all night. Here, on this lumpy mattress, and thin sheet. At home I have a
~~~~~~~~~~

seven thousand dollar mattress, fifteen hundred thread count Egyptian cotton sheets and I can't get to sleep before midnight. That's strange, in jail, and I slept like a baby, go figure!

The lady in the bottom bunk is telling me her name is Estelle. She says she is here because she lives in an apartment building that has limited parking spaces. She and a neighbor were arguing over a parking space. She pushed the woman, the woman fell. The woman's boyfriend was there and witnessed the episode and called the police. Of course the woman pressed charges.

Estelle is here for assault and battery. She could not believe she lost her temper and pushed the lady. She's tearing up telling me this. I climbed down from my upper bunk and took her hand and began praying for her. We were both crying when I finished praying. The guard is telling us its breakfast time and is waiting for us. As we left our cell, I was thinking, 'I wish all I had done was pushed someone down!'

My mind is still thinking about the word shame. After I eat, I'm going back to the cell to do more thinking.

Estelle is gone. Now I can lie on the bottom bunk again. I guess she made her phone call and someone put up her bail. I still can't bring myself to call anyone. I know Mom is worried sick trying to reach me. She probably has Mr. Williams worried too. I just can't phone her, I'm too humiliated. Too humiliated, now that reminds me of when I was in the third grade.

We were at the Shop Rite grocery store. I remember as we were getting in line to check out, I was thinking, 'here we go, getting in line.' Mom always makes the six of us come to the grocery store with her. She says we need to know how to be responsible, and shop in case she has to send us to the store. Stacey says it's because she is going to have another baby and when she has to stay inside the house, we need to know how to shop like she does.

Mom is very fussy about what brand of catsup and toilet paper she uses. Everything else lets just say it's sold if the price is right. Mom sure has a way of making grocery shopping fun though. At home, she writes out her list and posts it on the refrigerator. Each one of us gets to pick out an item, so we put our initials next to an item on the list and when we get to the grocery store, we know exactly what items we are to get.

I like to pick the cereal because the few times Ronnie picked it out, Clayton, Devin and Ronnie were the only ones that ate it. It was apparent that Captain Munch was as Ronnie put it, "The best cereal ever," only to little people under the age of seven. Mom fussed at Stacey, Janelle and I because we ate toast for breakfast and we ran out of bread before time to grocery shop again. After a couple times of running out of bread, Mom put my initials next to the cereal so now I have the honors of choosing it.

Stacey likes to pick the vegetables. She thinks because Mom lets her help cook, she is grown enough to pick vegetables. Sometimes she gets broccoli, and sometimes she gets cabbage; but, for sure she gets mixed vegetables, she loves them. Stacey gets the large, frozen family package and breaks out with this big grin as she sticks her chest out when Mom says to her, "Good choice Stacey, you are such a wise shopper." As we all watch Stacey put the mixed vegetables into the shopping cart, Janelle and Ronnie both turn up their noses as the bag goes down into the cart.

Janelle likes to pick the breads. She loves corn bread. If she had her way, we would eat it every day, even for breakfast. Mom says that's because when she was pregnant with Janelle she couldn't get enough corn bread, she even ate it for breakfast. Janelle also picks wheat bread, which no one likes but her. Whenever Stacey sees Janelle put wheat bread into the cart, she mouths out the word, "Boo gee." Janelle even slips cookie dough in the basket even though the cookie dough is usually the first item Mom puts back.

Ronnie now picks the toothpaste and makes good choices. In February, he'll be turning seven. Already he's hinting when his birthday comes, he'll start choosing the hot dogs. Stacey says he doesn't understand Mom gets the hot dogs that are on sale, but he'll find out soon enough.

Clayton sits in Stacey's cart and begs for everything he sees. Devin rides in Moms cart and holds, or should I say smashes, the toilet paper. He likes to make crashing sounds with it as he hits everything that comes within his reach. So, I really look forward to grocery shopping, that is until it's time to get in line to check out, this is the part I hate!

When Mom finds a line, no one likes to get behind us. We always have two full carts of food. Mom stands by the register and watches the prices as they're being entered and she keeps asking for a subtotal. Oh yeah, and she always, always has to put some things back. Whoever gets behind us in line; it never fails they all go through a series of sighs, changing their stance, rolling their eyes, looking several times at their watch, stretching their neck looking for the next shorter opened check out line, the whole exercise.

Each of us have our eyes on the food as it gets closer to the cashier with hopes nothing we picked will become a go back item as they call it. And I did mention Mom always has to put something back, always. As I stand in line I hope no one gets behind us but when they do, I watch them and watch out for the cereal and whatever else I want, to make sure it doesn't become a go back item.

This particular day, I was watching the cookie dough as it was nearing the cashier when suddenly I heard a lady in line behind us say, "Excuse me little girl, how old are you?" I turned around to see who the lady was talking to. She had her eyes fixed on me and added, "What grade are you in?" I noticed she was not alone, there was another woman standing next to her. They both looked to be in their fifties I'd guess, and their skin coloring, height and facial features were similar as though they could have been sisters.

Before I could say anything, Stacey blurted, "She's in the third grade, and she's in the fifth grade," pointing to Janelle, "and I'm in the seventh grade." Now having her finger on her chest, Stacey has extended her neck and it was wobbling from side to side and she had what Mom called "A tone" while telling the woman our grades. Now my eyes are locked on both women. As if they had rehearsed dance moves, they both raised their eyebrows and pulled on the collar of their clothes as if a draft had come their way.

They each took a step back and looked at one another. "How many kids do you think she has?" The other woman said. The woman who asked me the question looked towards Stacey and said in a real loud voice, "I don't know, but some people need to take birth control." Then she rolled her eyes and held her nose up in the air and turned her head away from our direction. Now, mind you I didn't know what birth control was then, but by the woman's tone and body language, I knew it was not good.

We all glanced over at Mom, knowing she was not letting that comment go without a reply. This time Mom had no words to blurt out. Her eyes bounced back and forth from one woman to the other. When she had their full attention, she made her eyes real small as if she could barely see out of them, then she poked out her mouth and put her hands on both sides of her big belly and began tapping her foot. She did this for about half a minute.

Suddenly, Mom stopped patting her foot, removed her hands from her sides, flattened out her lips, opened her eyes as big as she could get them, tilted her head slightly and began this slow motion, rolling of her eyes at them. I thought her eyes had bungee cords behind them, honest I did! I shuttered and thought to myself, 'man, she told them!' I glanced back at the women.

They looked at each other. The vocal one said, "No she didn't, let's find a shorter line with less people." They both put their noses up in the air as they walked away looking for another line.

You know, I didn't understand what I felt at that time, but those women caused me to feel humiliated. People like them made me feel embarrassed just because there were a lot of us. We may have lacked some material things but we NEVER lacked LOVE.

This is where my emotions get muddled. Mom always made us feel loved. I felt loved so much at home, within our four walls but outside the home and often, is where I would feel ashamed humiliated and degraded. I guess that's where my attachment with shame started, outside of my home... Maybe that's why it's so difficult for me to see how shame has an effect on me.

When I was young and would hear someone make a negative remark about a large family, I would think to myself, 'if only they could come home with me, they would see all of the love we share and the fun we have!' The older I became I felt as though I owed people an explanation as to why there were so many of us.

When Mom and I had our sex talk, she told me that God determines who will live. He was the author of life. Men and women are the vessels created to reproduce its own kind; human life. So, at home there was nothing wrong with there being so many of us, nothing to defend. We knew no other type of life.

As I became older, sometimes I felt I had to prove to people I didn't lack or suffer any lost because there were so many of us. But inside those four walls, Mom made us all feel loved and made sure we all affirmed our love for each other.

CHAPTER FIVE

Mom's Amazing Babies
Other people's opinion

Every time one of us had a birthday, we all had to gather in the kitchen around the table with the "Birthday Seat" at the head of the table, which was always closest to the stove. After placing the ice cream next to the cake on the table, Mom would begin telling the story of how happy she was the day the person sitting in the birthday seat was born.

Mom would fix her eyes on the birthday person and reminisce about where she was when she went into labor, what she was doing, who was there and her trip to the hospital. As soon as she started talking about her labor, she would slowly walk toward the birthday person and when she stood directly behind them, she'd gently slip her arms around them placing her cheek on their cheek, and she would describe how she felt when she was handed her amazing baby to hold in her arms for the very first time.

Mom always cupped her hand under the birthday person's chin, turn their face towards her, and express the emotion she felt the very first time she gazed upon the face of the baby she had talked to for the nine months she carried them. She would describe how the love in her heart would fill her eyes with tears as she tenderly kissed and held her amazing baby.

When I was little and it was my turn to sit in the birthday seat, I would giggle and twist in the chair so excited about being a year older. When I turned nine or ten, I would tear up when Mom removed her cheek from mine to turn my chin. I knew she loved me and to think of the very first time I was being held by her loving arms, just made me turn into Jell-O. After Mom would start to cry, the birthday person would give her a hug; and that was the cue for everyone in the kitchen to start singing the birthday song.

By the time I turned twelve, I realized, we all would grab napkins to dry our tears just before the turning of the chin. I can't explain it, but regardless of whose birthday, the love inside me would swell up for each one of my siblings. I would be so glad they were given life to become part of our big, loving family.

Maybe because Mom's love was so strong as she looked into the birthday persons eyes, it could be felt by everyone in the room. Or, because we each had a turn in the birthday seat, and we each knew the depth of love she had for who she always calls her "Amazing Baby" sitting in the seat. And no matter what disagreements we were having among ourselves, all it took was a birthday for us to realize we still loved each other.

After the birthday song we would all hug and tell one another, "I love you." Maybe the fact we each shared the same womb, and was held by the same loving arms, is the reason we share the same love for one another. Even now, Mom is always reminding us of each others birthdays. We don't do the cheek and chin routine anymore, but we all must be together for the birthday song.

Because Janelle lives in Detroit, and I live in Mableton, we do a conference call and have to be put on speaker phone. I always fly home, to Chicago for my birthday, April nineteenth. Now that it's only Devin and Sharon at home, sometimes Mom takes them to a restaurant and calls Stacey and has her call Ronnie and Ronnie calls Clayton and Clayton calls Janelle and Janelle calls me so we can all sing happy birthday together.

As a teenager, I wondered why Mom made such a big production out of our birthdays. We all had to be home before the festivities could begin, she insisted every one of us had to be present in the kitchen before we could begin the celebration and she always made all of our birthday cakes. What ever the birthday persons favorite color, that would be the color of the cake. Whatever the birthday person's favorite candy, Mom would pile the candy right on top of the frosting. What I can't comprehend is, how can a love that deep, a love that powerful, be threatened by shame? It just doesn't make sense to me.

Not long after I turned twelve, a classmate in my math class made a joke about a woman who had so many children, they didn't have names, they were called accrue (a crew). Again, the classroom resounded with laughter. Needless to say, I didn't laugh. I sat there remembering what that woman at the grocery store said about how some people need to use birth control and I myself wondered, why didn't Mom use birth control? I know birth control was available back then.

Now I'm laying here wondering if that's why I wrote those checks, knowing I shouldn't have. Maybe because at the time I wrote the checks I felt I deserved the clothes.

Am I ashamed of the fact there are so many of us and do I feel like I should be able to have what everyone else has. Or am I ashamed that there are seven of us and six different fathers. Maybe I'm ashamed of the fact people assume large families automatically suffer lack. And somewhere deep down in my heart I feel I must have everything I want just so I can prove to people that I lack nothing.

Maybe that's why I shop every Saturday; to prove I do not suffer lack. I don't know if one of these reasons made me write the bad checks or if all of these reasons combined made me write the bad checks. Oh, I do know being this transparent really hurts, I didn't realize I was suppressing so much pain. I usually spend hours and days reading but I have never sat this long and took inventory or examined myself to realize I am affected entirely too much by what other people think about me and my family.

Today is the first time I am able to see that peoples opinion of my family carries way too much weight with me. Umm, I guess that's been with me for most of my life because now I'm reminded of the day I have always referred to as my "Double Bam Day." The day I was kicked in the stomach with embarrassment twice. Can you believe that, twice in the same day.

The first bam I lied about not being hungry. I was in the eighth grade and it was sixth period. I was talking to Shauntel, Lakesha, and Marcus about our homework assignment. Mr. Morrison, our math teacher, had called off the names of us students he had grouped together for a project assignment. Knowing Mr. Morrison was such a stickler for detail, we were brainstorming about who was to research what as the bell rang. We each collected our things, and were talking and walking. We were so into our conversation. Before I realized it we ended up at the end of the hall. Knowing we each had different directions to go, we stood still and kept talking.

It was really very innocent, Marcus was the one who said, "Hey let's go to the Greeks and finish discussing this." The Greeks is the local hamburger hut two blocks from our school. All of the high school kids that drive, and the middle school kids from our school hang out there. It's popular among the school kids because the owner, Mr. Minos gives free fries on certain days to students who show their student ID card to the cashier. Because I didn't have money to go to the Greeks, I said, "Sorry, I'm really not hungry, you all go on, and I'll see you tomorrow in first period. Just let me know what you come up with."

I caught the glance they gave each other. They knew I was lying and didn't have any money. And what really, really did it; my stomach growled right at that precise moment. **BAM!** Talk about embarrassed! I felt my face turning red. I quickly turned around to leave and covered my stomach with my free hand as I made myself cross eyed once my back was turned to them, I was so embarrassed. To really make matters worse, I had to face them tomorrow and pretend nothing happened. Bam number one!

Stacey and Janelle were both in High School. The school busses had been discontinued in our area, so they had to take the city buses. Usually they get home an hour or so after me. My school is only six blocks away from where we live. Mom was working at the Coca-Cola factory then and most days she didn't get home until five-thirty or sometimes six p.m.. This is Ronnie's last year attending Elementary School with Clayton, Devin and Sharon. They all walk to and from school together and get home ten minutes after I do.

So, I am the first one home from school and my routine is; change out of my school clothes and make sandwiches for the five of us. Ronnie, Clayton, Devin and Sharon usually walk in the door as soon as I finish the last sandwich. The thing is, if I was late getting home, Ronnie would have to go to our neighbor, Ms. Sloan's apartment and get the key to our apartment so they could get in. Once they were secured inside Ronnie would reign over Clayton, Devin and Sharon. He would have them hanging his clothes up, putting his books in alphabetical order, getting him water, making him sandwiches, insisting they call him "King Ronnie," anything to prove he was in charge.

The few times I had been late, by the time I arrived home, Ronnie had them all in tears. So I always leave school right after the last bell so I won't be late getting home. After the five of us have our snack, we are to start our homework. If there is no homework from school, Mom has us read from books she makes us check out at the local library.

We write down on what Mom calls "The library check out list." Our name, the date, name of the book we are reading, and what page we ended on before we put the book back was what the list consisted of. Periodically, Mom would ask us questions about what we had read, and you couldn't make up stuff like Janelle tried to do once because Mom knew the storyline of each book.

Well, this day I was running late because of the time I spent in the hall talking, so I was almost jogging to get home. On my way home I was considering the fact of having to work with Shauntel, Lakesha and Marcus on this project and the odds of the subject coming up again about us all going to the Greeks. I was seriously thinking of what I could do to make some money so I'd be able to go the next time the Greeks suggestion came up.

Hey, I'm just now realizing, they never asked me again. Oh my goodness, how embarrassing is that. Even now, years later thinking about that embarrasses me, can it get any more embarrassing? Oh Lord help me with this please! I have got to let that go, Marva just drop the matter, girl let it go.

Anyway, I was almost home when the bright idea of sitting for our neighbor, Ms. Sloan came to mind. She had three small children and was always needing a babysitter because no one ever sat with them a second time. I knew how to handle them. I was just busy sitting my own younger brothers and sister. But to get some cash, I'd sit all seven of them together at the same time.

As I turned the corner to my street I looked up, oh NO! I saw Devin's father, Devin Green, Senior. My heart began to pound so fast, I thought it actually skipped a beat or two and I couldn't catch my breath. I stopped right where I stood. I stopped so fast, someone walking behind me walked into me. You see, Devin Senior is who I call, "The Peacock."

I decided to wait right where I stood until he left. He was just pulling up to the curb, parking that loud, orange and red stripped raggedy VW. He just had to gun the engine informing everyone on the whole block of his arrival. That's the peacock in him!

As I look up at the apartment building windows, I see curtains go back and heads peek out of the windows. **BAM!** Having my school books in one arm, I threw up my free arm and thought to myself, 'yeah give the peacock just what he wants, all eyes on him!'

He gets out of his car and flashes that gold tooth grin of his. He has gold on one of his front teeth in the shape of the state of Texas, yep the whole state on one tooth! Now I watch as he struts up towards our apartment building. I'm surprised he doesn't stop at the bottom of the steps and take a bow. Look at him, waving at everybody like he's top dog.

It is so embarrassing. I know his presence reminds everybody about Mom having seven kids and six different fathers and here comes one of the fathers now. Like it's any of their business. There is one good thing I can say about the peacock and that is, he does drop off some cash when he comes over. It's just his performances I could do without. I wish he would just buy some stamps, then I wouldn't be standing out here waiting for him to leave. I don't believe this, first the Greeks, now the Peacock **BAM, BAM!**

My goodness, I never realized I felt that way until now. I care entirely too much about what other people think. Why am I so embarrassed about Mom having so many kids? She has always taught us to love one another. Why is other peoples opinion so important to me? Lord please help me overcome these awful feelings of embarrassment, humiliation and shame. How do I rid myself of this shame that has become so much a part of me it's handicapping me?

This must be associated to my thinking I can write a bad check and it's acceptable. Did other people's opinion of me cause me to become irrational? Did I write those checks to buy clothes I wanted so I can look the part of not wanting for anything to other people?

Holy Spirit please show me how to resolve this issue I have. I'm beginning to realize I have concealed a lot of shame, a lot of humiliation and embarrassment. Reveal to me the root so I may yield as you pull it up and out of me. I am sorry for being so self centered and allowing what others think of me become the utmost of importance. I totally disregarded You had a reason for all of us to come into this world under the circumstances we did, and also the plans You have specifically for my life. Help me to walk in Your path. I will delight myself in Your way oh Lord. Thank you for my healing. Amen.

The guard has come for me. I'm off to the Chapel again tonight because I need more answers. She's telling me Pastor Houston is scheduled again for tonight. Oh that's great. I hope the woman who prayed for me last night is here again.

Ok it looks like I am the first person here for the service. I am really looking forward to this. I want to get prayer before I stand before the judge in the morning. I feel so much better since I've been thinking about this shame thing. I have never examined my childhood like this before, and I'm getting clarity about why some things happened the way they did. I can't express it in mere words but; deep in my inner man I feel like everything is going to be alright and something good is going to happen. Something for my good even though I'm in jail. Go figure!

That service was completely off the chart! Pastor Houston preached on abiding in the True Vine, Jesus. Pastor came from John 15:1-5, it states: ***"I am the true vine, and My Father is the Vinedresser. Every branch in Me that does not bear fruit He takes away: and every branch that bears fruit He prunes, that it may bear more fruit. You are already clean because of the word which I have spoken to you. Abide in Me, and I in you. As the branch cannot bear fruit of itself, unless it abides in the vine, neither can you, unless you abide in Me. I am the vine, you are the branches. He who abides in Me, and I in him, bears much fruit; for without Me you can do nothing".***

Tonight I learned being here in jail is a pruning process for me. I was headed in a direction that would have completely destroyed me. Not only was I not attending church, I was not connected to a covering at all and I am not bearing any fruit whatsoever. I was spiritually drying up like that vision I had of the lone piece of coal. I am so appreciative of the grace of God. He loves me so much He corrects me so I may get restored to The Vine again and bare fruit.

I'm reminded of Hebrews 12: 9 & 10, where the Word says if our earthly fathers correct us and we respect them for their correction, then, when we are corrected by the Lord, He is only trying to make us profit by taking on holiness, you know, the likeness of Him.

Then I thought being arrested just might be the best thing that could have happened to me. I have, for the first time in my life, taken a deep truthful inner look at myself. This is so strange, I am really glad I'm in jail! Oh I'm scared about what the judge will do to me. But I know I did wrong and I will have to take my punishment like a woman. I just know in my heart everything will work out for my good! Thank you Jesus!

CHAPTER SIX

Off To College Talk
Yanking that root out!

Oh my, my, my! Holy Spirit is so thorough! Now I think I understand where the root of my writing bad checks stemmed from. After service, when I walked into the cell, a copy of the court order was laying on my bed. Seeing it there took my mind immediately back to the day my acceptance into Spelman College arrived.

Stacey and Janelle were both away at college so Sharon and I shared the bedroom. It was a Saturday morning and after I had cleaned the bathroom I went into the bedroom to collect clothes for laundry and I saw an envelope lying faced down on my pillow. I picked it up and as soon as I flipped it over my eyes went to the return address. When I saw the college emblem I screamed, "I got it! I got my response from Spelman College." Ronnie, Clayton, Devin, and Sharon ran into the room bursting with anticipation along with mine.

Mom was cooking and had left the kitchen and was now standing in the doorway drying her hands off with her apron smiling and watching me. I started to tear it open but I was hesitant, my heart was pounding so fast I thought everyone in the room could hear it. I held the letter close to my heart and closed my eyes and said aloud, "Oh Lord, I do delight myself in you, let it be my hearts desire; let it be a yes." Mom eased into the room and slowly wrapped her arm around me and said, "Congrats Marva, how about just the two of us doing the laundry today, just you and me." As I opened my eyes and looked at her I said, "I haven't even opened it, it might be a dear Marva letter." She said, "Oh, you deserve Spelman baby, open and see." She was right, I was accepted!

After I read the letter aloud to everyone in the room, Sharon and I hugged then Ronnie, Clayton and Devin did a group hug with me and when they stepped away, I noticed Mom was exceptionally mute. I couldn't quite read her mood. She wasn't upset, she just wasn't herself. I thought, 'maybe she's going to tell me how much she'll miss me.' She cried for a solid week when Stacey left for Grambling College. And when Janelle left the state to go to Cosmetology School in Detroit, Mom cried for days.

Mom never let either one of them know she cried after they left. The day each of them left, Mom wrote down a day and time for them to phone her on a post it note and she watched them put it in their purse then she went into the kitchen and marked the kitchen wall calendar in large red ink. She would make sure to be home when Stacey called every Tuesday evening at eight p.m. and when Janelle left, her day to call was Mondays at eight p.m..

Mom asked each one of them to describe their rooms so she could get a visual of them studying. She always told them how proud she was they had earned scholarships to go to school. Mom would keep them abreast of what was happening here, with all of us. She would end every call with a prayer for their ability to stay focused on their school work and for their safety. She always ended her conversations with them saying, "Ok kiddo, make your Mom proud of her amazing baby, Love you."

After Janelle left, the first two or three phone calls I heard Mom say, "Why you couldn't go to school in the state of Illinois just doesn't make sense to me, but you did work hard and earned your way." About the fourth or fifth phone call, Mom never mentioned it again.

I could talk to Mom about anything and she never seemed uncomfortable talking to me about any subject, so I thought she was acting strange. As we walked to the Laundromat, I talked to her about what I wanted to take with me to Spelman. I was so excited. I was walking and talking I was so animated. She smiled but there was something about her, she just wasn't herself.

After we had all the clothes in washers, Mom bought us both an orange soda pop. She walked to the back of the room, sat down and motioned for me to come sit next to her. I thought, 'finally, she's going to tell me what day to call her and how much I'll be missed.' She twisted the top off her bottle, gave me a quick glance and directed her eyes back to the bottle as she got up and tossed the top into the nearby trash can. Then very slowly Mom walked back to me starring at her pop the whole time.

Mom sat down really close to me and took a long swallow of her pop followed by a deep sigh and as she lifted her eyes to mine she began saying, "Once upon a time, a girl named Cynthia was twenty years old, with two small amazing babies..." I thought oh lord, here we go again with another one of her "when you were an amazing baby" stories.

She continued saying, "With Stacey gripping tightly onto her skirt and Janelle's little arm clutched around her neck, she walked out of the grocery store after purchasing a few items, when suddenly Janelle's sip cup fell to the ground and rolled out of Cynthias' reach. Having her eyes fixed on the cup, she went scuttling right behind it. When the sip cup finally came to a halt, she bent over, extended her arm to pick it up and a big, strong, dark manicured hand reached for the cup one second before she did.

Cynthia looked up and directly into the biggest darkest brown eyes, and time stood still for what seemed like five minutes. All of a sudden Janelle let out a loud "Mine" and time started again. They smiled at each other and both say at the same time, "Sorry." He told her it was no bother, it was apparent she could use another pair of hands and he just happened to have an extra pair.

He gently took the bag of groceries from her arm, and began to walk with her. It seemed like just a few moments had gone by before she realized they had arrived in front of her apartment building. Mom says after that day, he would show up outside her apartment, to be there for her in case she needed to get groceries. He was so kind and such a gentleman. He never asked to come into her apartment, nor did he pressure her about which unit she lived in. This man was my father, Malcolm Harris.

She told me since I would be going off to college; she wanted me to be cautious and aware of men who are not sincere about lasting relationships. She did not want me to fall prey as she had. My father was married, with four sons. At the time they met, he had been separated from his wife for three months and was staying in a condo just one block from her apartment.

He was a corporate attorney, and had been one for five years. Because his job demanded long hours his four sons were beginning to show signs of being deprived of a full time Dad. Both he and his wife agreed that after ten years of marriage, he had primarily spent most of his time at school or work; the separation was mutual. He needed some time alone to determine where his priorities should exist.

Three months into her relationship with Malcolm, Mom discovered she was pregnant with me. The night she told him she was pregnant, he told her he and his wife were getting back together to try and make the marriage work. He said he would pay for her to go to a doctor, he wrote her a check she never cashed, placed it on the coffee table and he walked out.

Almost every day for the next four months, Malcolm would be dressed in jogging outfits, running in place at the corner watching for her. She thought he would approach her and ask if they could still keep seeing each other and she was so vulnerable she thought it was best she moved. She could never get rid of any of us because we were all conceived out of love. That's why she always calls us her "Amazing Babies."

Amazing? Did she say amazing? I was so angry! I didn't know if I should slap her, flick my orange pop on her face, or place my head on her shoulder and cry. I was so hurt and angry and strolling right behind those emotions comes confusion up in my mind. Because of what Mom has just told me, now I have all these questions popping up in my head. I asked, "Did he die before or after I was born?" She said, "Marva, what makes you think your father died?"

I said, "When I was little, I overheard you telling someone he was dead." She says to me "Baby, your father did not die." I leaped straight up out of my seat and even though I stood there staring at her with my eyes; like pages in a book being flipped over by a strong gust of wind, my mind was recalling past conversations trying to figure out why I never knew he was alive.

I slightly bent over towards her face and yelled, **"He's not dead! You mean he's alive? My father has been alive all this time and you didn't tell me anything about him all these years?"** Mom looked me directly in the eyes and softly said, "I wanted you to be happy about your life, and not be distressed about having a father that did not want to include you in his." I bent all the way down and got in her face, squinted my eyes and replied, "Mom, how do you know that, he might have wanted to know who I was, what I looked like, he might have changed his mind after he saw me. It was wrong for you to keep me from my father, Mom, just wrong."

Her eyes watered and she stood up, reached for the back of my head and pulled me to her. With my face buried on her shoulder; she hugged and rocked me while I cried. She tenderly says, "Because of the circumstances involving your father's wife and sons, baby I never wanted him to resent neither me nor you for causing his marriage to break up. Malcolm obviously loved his wife and because I loved him with such a deep love, I chose to let him go and be happy with his wife and sons."

Mom pulled me slightly away from herself and looking up, trying to make me look directly into her eyes, she told me with tears in hers that as far as she was concerned, she gained me out of their relationship. I was the remnant she had of him, a part of him she would always have to love.

She guided me to sit next to her. She said when I was about six or seven years old, I stopped asking her about my father and because I never asked about him, she never brought him up. She noticed it's been years since I pulled out the pictures in our family photo album to look at her and Malcolm's pictures together so she thought I was okay with him not being an active part of my life.

She figured today was the best time to tell me the story of how her and Malcolm met and the circumstances regarding my being conceived. She wanted me to avoid the same type circumstances, and she understood my wanting to know my father and my being upset. If I wanted her too, she would help me find him. I told her I really needed to think about it. I didn't say anything else to Mom after that. I was so angry with her for keeping my father from me.

We sat silently waiting on the clothes to finish washing and I fought back tears a few times thinking about how Mom was the thread that kept me from my father all of my life. Then my imagination kicked in.

Scene number one, I saw Mom pregnant with me standing at the cash out counter of the local drug store. When she turns around to leave, Malcolm is standing there. He was so glad to see her; he hugs her and rubs her stomach. He tells her he loves her more than his wife and is getting a divorce and asks Mom to marry him. She says yes and they walk away together.

The next scene I saw Mom in the hospital in labor with me. In runs Malcolm, asking everyone at the front desk where is Cynthia Montgomery because she was having his baby and he loved her and wanted to be there to see his baby being brought into this world. Then he walks into the room where Mom is, the nurse brings me in, Malcolm asks to hold me and when the nurse puts me in his arms, he asks Mom to marry him and she says yes. I had various images of Malcolm asking Mom to marry him and she smiles each time and says "Yes."

Then I saw us, Mom, Malcolm, Stacey, Janelle and me, as a family. After I thought about it I added Ronnie, Clayton, Devin and Sharon, but Malcolm was their father now. I imagined all of us dressed in white slacks and navy blue tops, on a yacht, with servants waiting on us. I saw us all living in a big two story house with a lot of expensive furniture. I saw myself with my own car, a sixteenth birthday present from Mom and Dad: a candy apple red, Mercedes SLK convertible. And I looked so good in it!

When the clothes were done being washed Mom and I placed them in dryers and again we waited in silence. I started thinking again, this time about Mom and her amazing baby's daddy's and how it would have been nice if the daddy's had been amazing. Sterling Townsend, Stacey's father, was killed in the military before she was born. James Lott, Janelle's father was a drummer in a local band and was discovered by a record company and left Chicago on a tour that never ended. My father, Malcolm Harris, already married, walked out when he found out about my impending arrival. Then there's Herman Addison, Ronnie and Clayton's father.

Herman Addison was the only positive image I had of a father. I was just a year old when he met Mom and he always treated me like I was his daughter. I thought he was my father until Mom sat me down with the family picture album and pointed out Malcolm Harris and told me he was my father, and that Herman loved me like my father. Herman was the only man that stayed in Mom's life for any length of time, five years.

They met when he delivered a package to Mom. At that time Herman was working for a large overnight delivery company. When Mom came to the door, I was only a year old at the time and she had me in her arms. Stacey was almost five and Janelle was getting ready to turn three and they were full of energy. While she was signing for her package, she kept telling the two of them to stop jumping off the sofa. He noticed how she was struggling with three little girls and a few days later he left two toy dolls outside the front door with a note that read, "*For the two future Olympic jumpers, signed, the delivery man.*"

After that day Herman would buy a toy for one of us every payday, always leaving the toy outside the front door with a note. After a few months of accepting toys from Herman, Mom left him a note stating what time he could bring any future toys by.

Herman and Mom begin dating and a month later she was pregnant with Ronnie. Herman had been taking business and college courses and he completed them not long after Ronnie was born. That's when he started his own delivery service and a few months later he proposed to Mom and would propose every week. Just before Ronnie turned two Clayton arrived and Herman kept proposing to Mom until Clayton's second birthday party that was the last time he asked for her hand in marriage.

We all thought Mom and Herman were going to get married. To this day, some of my best childhood memories are when Herman was in our lives. He took us to the beach and to parks, and some Sunday's he would pick us up and take us all to church.

Laying here now remembering how Herman would show up some Friday evenings with groceries, pizzas, barbecue or Chinese food and he always left wads of money, those memories puts a smile on my face. I remember holding onto Hermans' leg begging him to stay whenever he would head for the door to leave.

I thought Herman made a good father and he loved Mom so much. The way he looked at her and how he would listen to what she had to say with all of his attention on her; you just knew he loved him some Cynthia. But Mom said Herman knew it was impossible for him to take care of five children and a wife. With him just starting a business, marriage would be adding unnecessary stress upon what he already had to handle.

I was so disappointed and missed Herman terribly when he stopped spending time with us during the week. I guess he couldn't stand to see the disappointment in our eyes whenever he had to leave so he stopped coming over all together.

When Ronnie and Clayton were older Herman signed them both up for all kinds of sports and he would pick them up and take them to all the practices and games but he would never hang around. Whenever he would call on the phone for Ronnie or Clayton he always had them tell me, "Dad says hi and he loves you." Herman faithfully mailed his child support and, should Ronnie or Clayton need anything outside his payments, it was there pronto, via his delivery company.

Next was Devin Green Senior, the peacock contractor. I don't think I have ever liked him and not because he so happened to have followed Herman. He is such a show off, flashy and always making promises he has no intentions of keeping. He never had nor has intensions of marrying anyone. Every other word out of his mouth is, "Hey now baby" and as young as I was I noticed if you were in conversation with him and another woman walked by, his head always follows the woman walking by and "Hey now baby" has a way of just sliding out of his mouth.

Mom met him while she was working at "Fast Blinds Manufacturing." Business was booming and the shipping department, where she worked, was busting out at the seams so the owner hired a contracting company for expansion and improvements. Devin Senior was the foreman and while the men were working, something fell right through Mom's assembly station and Devin had to write up the report of how and what happened so headquarters would reimburse Mom's company for the damage. He really pushed himself on her, she tried to brush him off but he kept pursuing her.

They only dated for about eight or nine months. They had already broken up when Devin was born. The only good thing I can say about Devin Senior is he makes sure my brother wants for nothing. He's a good provider I have to give him that. And Devin tells us he has a younger brother that his father takes care of also.

Now Sharon's father, Shawn McCullough, was around for almost two years. Mom met him in the bank while cashing her check. Of course it was Friday and the line was so long they struck up a conversation and he waited for her and gave her a ride home. He was a very quiet man, a man of few words. When we would all get together, you would never know Shawn was in the room.

Sometimes I would watch him interact with Mom. They would sit for hours and never exchange dialogue. I often wondered why she even dated him.

Most of the time all he would say was hello and good bye. He did smile a lot though. He ended up in prison on assault charges.

One day he was at a gas station, in line to pay for his gas. A man came in and stepped up to the front counter, just cut the line where everyone else was waiting. Shawn was the only person to say anything to the man. The man told Shawn he was in a hurry.

Shawn told him everybody in line was in a hurry and he needed to get in the back of the line. After that, there were different versions of what happened. The trial was in the local newspaper every day and we all kept abreast of it. When the cashier testified, he said the man appeared to pick up his arm towards Shawn, and Shawn hauled off and cold cocked him.

The man hit the floor and never got up. Apparently when he hit the floor his brain swelled and the fall rendered him comatose for over a year. The only lady in line said the man was just turning around towards Shawn and before he could balance himself, Shawn hit him. Two other men in line said Shawn was protecting himself; the guy was going to hit him. Just before the trial ended the man recovered from the coma. So Shawn was found guilty of assault.

While at the Laundromat; after my assessment of our not so amazing fathers, I thought, 'Mom was just trying to help me by warning me not to fall for the same type men she had.' So I felt just a little better about her telling me the story of her and Malcolm Harris. Then I was mad at her for not telling me my father was not dead, I might have had a relationship with him.

The more I thought about that, I realized Mom knows me and my imagination and how I would have looked him up and may have even tried to contact him. Then I realized Mom was right by keeping me from knowing he was alive. It was his choice not wanting us in his life; the life he was trying to hold together for his wife and sons. After all in his mind, I was just a mistake! The thought of how he didn't want me made me furious and I became angry towards Malcolm Harris, huh, who needs him anyway!

When the clothes were dry, we folded them, put them in containers and walked home still silent. I saw Mom looking at me several times, but she didn't say anything and I was glad. When we walked in the apartment I went straight to my room. I put my clothes up, closed the door and laid across my bed and started thinking about what Mom had just told me.

Now I'm wishing Mom had never told me my father was alive, at least when he was dead he loved me. And not only is he alive, my goodness he's married! How shameful I felt knowing I was an unwanted, "love child." Lord, why would you allow me to be conceived out of an affair and, be deceived for seventeen years! Why didn't Holy Spirit reveal to me about Malcolm Harris; I felt like a total idiot.

I remembered why I thought Malcolm Harris was dead all these years. I had just started the second grade and Mom took me with her to parent and teacher conference. While we waited in line for her to talk to my teacher, my classmate Shayla

Jackson and her Mom were in line behind us. Mom and Ms. Jackson struck up a conversation, when we left my class, we stopped by the office. As we were walking out of the office, Ms. Jackson and Shayla were walking to the parking lot and offered us a ride home. As it turned out, we lived only a few blocks from each other.

A few weeks later, Janelle had to leave school early and Mom had Ms. Jackson drop me off at home after school. I remember both rides because Ms. Jackson had a long black car with power windows and soft cloth seats. Herman was the only other person whose car I had rode in and his car had towels in the seat and the windows were not automatic. Normally we always walked or caught the bus every where we went so I was very happy to ride in a car that pretty again.

After Ms. Jackson dropped me off, I ran upstairs and when I looked in the hiding place for the key to get into the apartment, it was gone. I tried the door knob; it was unlocked. I thought it was strange if Mom is home why did Ms. Jackson pick me up from school? When I stepped inside our apartment, I could hear a woman's voice that was not familiar to me. Mom seldom has company so as I walked towards the kitchen, I listened.

The lady was saying something about Malcolm Harris. Then I heard Mom tell this lady that she didn't talk about Malcolm Harris because he was no longer with us. The woman asked, "Sickness?" Mom said, "No, automobile accident." I thought at that moment that's why I have never seen him; only pictures of him and Mom together. By then I was standing at the kitchen door. Mom introduced me to the lady and told me to go and change my clothes.

While changing my clothes, I began to fantasize about my father being slumped over the steering wheel, of a long, black beautiful automobile like the one I had just had a ride in. My father's car is in the real busy intersection up the street; Blaine and Baltimore. Someone passing by runs to the car and tries to rescue my father. When they swing the car door open, Malcolm Harris slightly lifts his head from the steering wheel and as he gasps for breath he manages to say, "Tell Marva that daddy loves her." Then he slumps over and dies.

That was my fantasy for years, the car would change but my father would always take his last breath loving me. Now I find out he's not even dead and, he didn't even want me! I'd rather believe my fantasy instead of the truth. The nerve of him not wanting me and the thought of him writing a check for me to disappear has me way, way past fuming! He's alive and living right here in Chicago. When I calmed down, my imagination started again.

I saw myself as I stepped into an elevator and pushed the floor I wanted. Someone taps me on my shoulder, I turn to see who it is, and there stands my father Malcolm Harris. He asks me if my mother's name is Cynthia. He begins to tell me how he knew I was his daughter because I was a splitting image of her. I had fantasy after fantasy and in each one; my father would always know I was his child.

Then I wondered could I have possibly been in the same places as my father? What if I had been in line at the post office at the precise time he was? The thought of him being alive and I could have walked right by him made me mad all over again.

Then I really felt bad. How can I tell anyone the truth now, after all these years he's been dead. That is too humiliating, and what about the fact he didn't even want me? I guess five kids was one more too many for Mr. Attorney Malcolm Harris! He had a good job, lawyers make bank for what I understand. His money really could have helped around here and what about my brothers?

What if I happened to meet one of them? My very existence is shameful. Now I'm thinking about the women in the grocery store again, I'm wondering myself, why didn't she just use birth control? Oh lord, I'm so ashamed of how I got here!

The next day we all went to church and I was still distant towards Mom. The Sunday School lesson was on Exodus 15:22-27, about how Moses brought the children of Israel from the threatening Red Sea into the wilderness and they went to Marah and when they arrived there the water was so bitter they couldn't drink it.

The people complained against Moses and Moses cried out to the Lord and was instructed to cast a tree into the water and the water was made sweet. The Lord spoke to Moses and told him to tell the people if they will just trust and obey Him the life he had prepared for them was good, healthy and prosperous.

After listening to the Sunday School story I thought, 'Mom was like Moses; telling me about my father and that puts me in a bitter place. I really had no intensions of staying angry at her. What I had to do was digest this information and not be upset at the messenger.'

Our Sunday School teacher Sister Manning, said, "Had the children of Israel changed the way they viewed God and His commandments, they would have lived a life of ease." A bell went off inside me and I realized what Mom always says, "God is the author of life! I was born for a purpose." I should focus on my purpose and not on the fact my father did not want me.

After Sunday School was dismissed, I found Mom and told her I loved her and hugged her really tight. She hugged me and looked deeply into my eyes and smiled.

Oh my, I don't believe this! Oh my goodness! I realize just now, this very instant, that my worship changed then. Oh my goodness! I became extremely angry at God for allowing me to be born through an affair. I remember that night after Mom told me about Malcolm Harris, right before I went to bed, I said my prayers and when I began to pray in the spirit; I was hesitant. I remember thinking to myself: 'How could God the Father love me when my own father didn't?' Before that day, Herman was my measurement of a father's love for me.

After the Laundromat I began to doubt if I could totally trust God. After all He never revealed to me my father was not dead. I kinda backed off when it came time to surrender my all to Holy Spirit after that day. I would question whether or not Holy Spirit would really tell me all things and if I could really have the mind of Christ. I felt really stupid having all the power available to me from the spirit realm and then find out how Holy Spirit deliberately kept my fathers existence from me.

I thought about all the people I had told in my past my father had died when I was little and I never had a chance to know him. I felt so foolish and betrayed by Holy Spirit; Who I had trusted all my life... Until now...

Today as I reminisce, I realize after the Laundromat I would get moved by praise and enter into worship, but I developed a resistance. I didn't enter into worship totally yielded and uninhibited as before. I just didn't trust Holy Spirit like I did before. It was the day I found out about Malcolm Harris not wanting me; that was the day my worship no longer increased. I operated on "Auto Pilot Mode," when it came to my worship time.

My goodness! That's why I never complained about not being able to go to church anymore. That's why it was so easy for me to turn off my alarm clock on Saturday's; I knew in my heart I wasn't getting closer or more intimate with Holy Spirit. My Lord, my Lord, heal me please this is so painful... I can not stop crying...

As I sob, I see how for the first time since the off to college talk, I am establishing the truth; the truth of how the shame in me took deeper roots and slowly and completely choked out my relationship with the

Lord and hindered my spiritual growth; and I let it! Now I see why it was so easy for me to gradually slip away from the intimate relationship I had. All because I felt betrayed by Holy Spirit...

Oh I repent now of feeling betrayed and for shutting You out of my heart. Oh my; I truly repent for not trusting You to know what was best for me and I am so sorry for accusing You of causing me shame.
I surrender wholeheartedly to You and give You permission to remove all of the shame and its affects from me. Holy Spirit I ask You to replace the unhealthy with healthy and give me an understanding that I may forgive. In the Mighty Name of Jesus I pray, Amen.

CHAPTER SEVEN

Amazing Babies Daddies
Oh, the hurt in truth!

Lord I thank You for forgiving me! Your ways are so beyond figuring out. Oh how I bless Your Wonderful Name! I'm glad I was arrested and have the time to examine myself. Let me continue reflecting and maybe, hopefully I'll find more truth and become totally free!

Ok where was I? Ooh this is so good. Let me see, oh yeah after church we ate and after we cleaned the kitchen Mom said she was going out for a while and she'd be back in a few hours. I decided to phone Stacey and then Janelle while Mom was gone and tell them what I had just been told about my father. I wanted to find out if Mom had the same conversations with them before they left for college.

I phoned Stacey first and she told me when she was around ten or eleven years old, she asked Mom about her father. Mom told her he was a good man and he was very happy about becoming a father. Before she left for college, Mom asked Stacey if she had any questions about her father. Stacey asked Mom how did they meet. Mom told Stacey she and Sterling were high school sweethearts. They were both seniors and around the month of April, before their graduation, Sterling had an argument with his Dad about his future.

Sterling was very smart and had a scholarship to any college of his choosing. Mom and Sterling had planned to go to college together. He wanted to become a football coach, and she wanted to become a social worker. His Dad wanted him to go to college and become an architect; his Dad grounded him for disagreeing with him. The only place Sterling was allowed to go was to school and home. No football practice, no Cynthia, just school and home.

The next day at school, Mom noticed Sterling was acting strange. He was so mad at his father for wanting to control his future. After lunch Mom saw Sterling between classes, and he told her he was not going to let his father have the last say, he had a plan. Sterling waited until school was over and walked all the way to the nearest recruitment center and joined the United States Marines. Three days after graduation, Sterling left for boot camp. Before he left Mom and Sterling had sex for the first time. He went to boot camp and came home to find her pregnant.

They planned on getting married when he returned on his next leave. Mom, her sister; Aunt Laura and his mother Grandma Tina were planning the wedding. Two months before Stacey was born, he was killed in action. Sterling's parents grieved the death of their only child awfully hard. His father blamed himself and his mother afflicted more harm accusing him of taking her only baby from her. Sterling Senior died less than a year later from grief and a broken heart. Grandma Tina buried her husband and moved back to Tennessee to live with her relatives. Grandma Tina; as we all called her kept in touch with us and spoiled Stacey tremendously.

When Stacey turned twenty-one she received a large trust fund from her grandparents. Because

Mom was not married to Sterling when he died, she nor Stacey was entitled to any of his military benefits. Stacey told me after Mom talked to her about Sterling, Mom went on to tell her how much potential she saw in her and did not want Stacey to let any man stop her from achieving all she had to do.

After we talked, Stacey prayed for me. She prayed I would be healed of not being wanted and for love and forgiveness to flow in and through me. After we finished our conversation, I sat for a few moments, allowing Holy Spirit to move in my heart. I was really hurt having to come to grips with the fact the father I spent seventeen years fanaticizing loved me; didn't. I needed Stacey's prayer to really penetrate my heart. I was so way pass hurt; I almost didn't feel anything but anger.

Then I called Janelle knowing she had talked to Mom about my getting accepted at Spelman College. When she answered the phone, I said, "Janelle, I need to talk to you." She laughed and said, "Don't tell me, you and Mom went to do the laundry right?" Janelle told me she remembers asking Mom about her father, James Lott when she was in the second or third grade. Mom told her about the wonderful man he was. But just like me, before she left for college, she and Mom went to the Laundromat and bam, she found out about James Lott, the person. Mom told her he was the kind of man that could say hello to a woman and captivate her heart.

Mom had just started working at the shipping yard as an inventory clerk. It was her second week working and early one morning while she was sitting at the bus stop on her way to work this bright red two door car pulled up abruptly right in front of the bus stop.

The front passenger door flew open and out of it staggers this tall skinny very cute black man. He was wearing a light brown cap, a shinny lime green wide lapel shirt, dark brown wide legged casual pants and lime green nylon socks with lime green croc shoes. The woman driving shouts at the man now lying on the ground telling him to lose her number. She leans over and grabs the car door shut, and gets rubber as she takes off.

The man gets up, dusts himself off, and steps up on the sidewalk. In a deep radio announcer type voice he says, "Well good morning everyone, it looks like I'll be riding the bus with you all this fine morning." Mom thought he was drunk at first, but he stood behind her and all she could smell was his cologne.

When the bus arrived, it just happened he sat next to her. Mom has excessive eye blinking. She blinks constantly and to keep James Lott from interpreting her excessive eye blinking as flirting, she never made eye contact with him. He began telling her he was sorry for his grand entrance. He was in a band called, "Rhythm and Hues" which explained the clothes he was wearing and, he and the lady that literally dropped him off had a terrible misunderstanding.

Mom never said anything. She put her back to him so he would get the hint she could care less. That was her first mistake; James liked women he had to pursue. For the next month, James Lott would ride the bus and if anyone was sitting next to her, he would tell them he was working on something, and had to sit next to her. Everyone he told that line to would just get up and move. Every time he did this, Mom would get up and move away from him. He would sit near her and start talking to her. If the bus was crowded, he would stand close to her and talk.

Mom told Janelle that James had a way about him. When he talked to you, you felt as though you were the only person in the room with him. He told her since he didn't know her name he was going to call her, "Miss Bus Stop." The second week he rode the bus, she told him she was married and was not interested in him. He never said anything he just looked at her and smiled. By then, everyone on the bus knew all of his business and was calling her Miss Bus Stop.

James Lott was twenty two years old, six feet four and played basketball in school. He earned a scholarship so he could study music in college. He was the drummer in his band; he didn't drink alcohol nor used any drugs. He shared an apartment with the bass guitar player in his band. After he told all there was to tell about himself, he would start talking about his gig the night before.

The fourth week of riding the bus he asked Mom if there was anything she wanted to know about him, he said to her, "Anything you want to know I'll tell you, just ask me, go ahead, ask." She was sitting in a seat in front of him so she turned around and asked him why he never talked about his family. She said he looked totally shocked she would ask him that. He got up and sat next to her and he turned very serious.

He told her his father was a Preacher and his mother was the typical First Lady and they disowned him because they said he plays the devil's music. He was the only child and he understood how disappointed they must be, however he had to live his own life and make his own choices just as they had. Still talking, he got off the bus with Mom that day and walked with her to the shipyard. He asked her what time she get off work. She told him four-thirty. When her shift ended, she walked out of the shipyard and there he was sitting on the hood of a late model Ford, F150 truck.

When he saw her, he climbed into the truck and drove to where she was. He put the truck in park and jumped out to open her door and asked if she had a good day. Mom asked where did he get the truck from. He told her it was his; he was only taking the bus so they could get to know one another. He knew she was a lady and would never let him pick her up. She asked to see his driver's license and registration before getting into the truck. Everything checked out and she let him take her to the sitters; she had to pick up Stacey. Stacey fell in love with him and Mom felt comfortable letting him drop her off in front of her apartment.

After that day, he would pick her up from work, they would get Stacey and he would take the three of them to dinner every day she worked. After dinner he would drop Mom and Stacey off and go do his band thing. This was their dating routine for several months then she asked him to attend church with her and Stacey. One Sunday he slid into the seat next to her, red eyed and all. After they knew each other for six months, James started talking about marrying her. He told Mom the band was going on tour and when he returned he wanted to get married.

Mom believed he was serious about getting married so she started having sex with him. That was her second mistake. He left on a two month tour and while he was gone, she discovered she was pregnant. After the tour ended he arrived at the shipyard to pick her up. She had planned to tell him about being pregnant when they started planning their wedding. Three weeks later she realized there wasn't going to be a wedding. Two months later she started to show.

One evening they were at a restaurant, after she ordered her meal, he asked, "Miss Bus Stop, don't you think you might need a salad, because you seem to be picking up some weight." She told him, "All I need is a daddy for your baby I'm carrying." Mom said as dark as he was, he went stone white.

It took James Lott about fifteen minutes before he could move. He sat staring at Mom even after the food was brought to the table. The waitress came to him and asked if something was wrong with his order and he snapped out of his daze. He picked over his food and when they finished eating he took her and Stacey home.

Before Mom stepped out of the truck, James told her while he was on tour a recording company offered the band a contract. He was giving some serious thought to signing it. He said he was going to take care of the three of them. But he did not want to be tied down right at that time because he had to be able to travel with the band.

Mom wanted to believe him, but her heart was telling her not too. They kept the dating routine up until a few weeks later when he left Chicago. He phoned her at work and told her to meet him at the train station at five thirty. She said after talking to him she didn't have a good feeling about meeting him. When her shift ended, she called for a cab to the train station instead of taking the bus and she waited for him.

James arrived with boxes piled a mile high, right then she knew he had no intentions of returning to Chicago. He didn't see her, but she saw him walking towards the ticket booth. A few seconds later here comes this tall, thin model looking woman, running to catch up with him and she slipped her arm in his. He looked around the station and said something to her. She dropped her arm from his and stood where she was, letting him walk away from her.

Mom walked up to him and asked was Cynthia just another name penciled in his black book? Did he ever have any intensions of marrying her or returning to Chicago? He couldn't look her in the face, he sheepishly said, "Come on Cynthia, I promise I'll be back to get the three of you in a few weeks, baby, come on!" But she wasn't buying it. She had already seen the other woman. He kept looking away from her acting nervous.

When it was announced to board for Memphis, Tennessee, James slipped his arms around her waist, held her close and with tears in his eyes said, "Baby, I'm going away for two, three weeks at the most, and when I come back I'll get all three of you, I promise." She forced his grip from her, turned around and walked away never looking back as tears streamed down her face all the way to the bus station.

Now she had two babies to feed.

Janelle told me she was so mad at Mom for letting her think her father was this loving, caring person. It took her almost a week to realize Mom was just protecting her. She told me to hang on in there, and that I'll cool off soon. Then she prayed for me.

After talking to Janelle I thought, 'she had a father that didn't want her in his life and she turned out just fine.' Janelle makes good money and at that time she was seeing Guy Carson, a night club owner in Detroit. I can do the same thing. I'll prove to Mr. Attorney Malcolm Harris he did me a favor not wanting me.

I was going to get what was taken from me, all by myself! I was going to make up for everything I missed out on growing up without his money. I was not going to listen to any sweet talk, or get involved with any man. I had to accomplish my goal of living a good life, and nothing in this world was going to stop me. I was so angry; angry at Mom for falling in love with losers, and angry at my father the lawyer, who refused to accept one more child.

I was so diligent in college because I wanted to make a lot of money. I changed my major twice and only chose to become an accountant because of the potential to make a lot of money impressed me. I think I understand now, I write personal checks on money that I don't have, not caring what the consequences are as long as I can buy what I want. Proving to myself and Malcolm Harris I turned out just fine without him and, "I am not deprived because he wasn't a part of my life. And despite what *he* thinks, I am somebody and my life does matter, even if it doesn't matter to him!"

I remember praying that night after talking to Stacey and Janelle and asking the Lord to give me strength and the ability to make excellent grades in college that I might become wealthy.

Lord this hurts... I really do care that Malcolm Harris did not want me... I do care that he never tried to find out if Mom aborted me or not... I do care that I was conceived out of an affair. I do care that I am illegitimate, I do care, and it does bother me it really does... I can't control my sobbing......oh God! Help me, this hurts, this really does hurt!... I can't stop crying... oh the pain... Forget it I'll just let it all out!.......**Oh God help me!**

I need to be healed and forgive my father for not wanting me... Holy Spirit heal me! This hurts so much, oh this sobbing won't stop... now snot is flowing uncontrollably and I'm shouting! **"Lord I'm sorry for hating my father, I'm sorry for being angry with him and hating him for loving my brothers more than he loved me. I'm sorry for hating him for loving his wife more than Mom.**

I simmer down but continue; Forgive me for being so hateful. I am so sorry and I do apologize for the anger and hate I harbored towards him Lord... and towards You. I need this to be removed from me NOW!"

Oh, oh this hurts. I have got to get some tissue. I guess I'll just have to use this sheet. I repent Lord and accept the truth; the truth is I held onto anger and hate to cover my feelings of rejection and shame. And the truth about being upset with You for keeping it from me, Oh Lord I'm so sorry...

Now that I have totally simmered down, I realize this is so easy for me to see now that I am in jail.

Not being busy but being still long enough to take inventory and examine myself. I need to forgive Mom; she could have easily aborted me. Instead she loved me and shielded me from the pain of knowing my father did not want me. And now I'm thinking of Mr. Herman Addison; what a loving heart he must have to love another man's child.

Herman always called me "M and M" like the candy. He always bought me presents for my birthdays, an outfit for Easter, and one toy and an outfit on Christmas. When he would take Ronnie and Clayton shopping for school clothes, he would always make sure I had two outfits and the receipt would always be in the bag in case I wanted to exchange them. Whenever he would send money by delivery, he'd sign the card, "For: Marva, Ronnie and Clayton."

When Herman found out I was leaving for college, he sent me two hundred dollars via his delivery service the morning I left headed to the bus station, Spelman bound. He slipped a handwritten note inside that read, "M & M; do good and good will come back to you. Always, HA."

Thinking about this now, Mr. Herman Addison always made me feel he took the place of my father. Now, I must be appreciative and thankful to him for stepping up to the plate to pinch hit for Malcolm Harris. What a loving heart Mr. Herman Addison must have. Lord I thank You for having Herman Addison as a father figure for me when I needed it most. Lord thank You, You are so wise.

And my father, I must forgive him. At least for being honest. Instead of sticking around just to resent me and abuse me either verbally or physically or possibly both. He left me alone and the Lord sent Mr. Addison in his stead.

Lord, I thank you for revealing to me the root of my shame, and the embarrassment, anger, hurt and hatred attached to it. I need your grace to cover me while I work at forgiving my parents, and replacing my un-forgiveness with love and understanding. Holy Spirit, help me, show me what I need to do so I can correct the wrong I've done.

I also repent for being consumed about what other people think of me, and for making my life's quest proving to others that I am somebody. Lord I am very sorry, I regret the wrong I've done. I'll tell the judge that I will pay for the clothes and do community service on weekends until my bill is satisfied. Thank you Jesus! Thank You!

Now I hope my loving family can forgive me for putting them through so much worry and anxiety. Let me go call Mom, and tell her what happened.

I called for the guard and she allowed me to make my phone call. After Mom cried she told me everyone was worried sick and that Janelle had started a prayer chain, and Mr. Williams was sleeping with his front door open, so he could hear me whenever I came home. They thought I was involved in an automobile accident and was unable to phone anyone.

Both Mom and Mr. Williams had phoned the Mableton police and were told the same thing; forty eight hours had to expire before the local police could investigate my being missing.

I told Mom what happened to me and how I rededicated myself to the Lord. Also how I intend to face the judge in the morning and take my spanking like a big girl. I asked her to forgive me for being so angry towards her for keeping my father from me.

After I told her everything, she told me she has been praying for me every since she told me about my father. The chip on my shoulder was very obvious to her. Something had to happen to make me come to the conclusion this world does not care one way or another about me and she was glad I didn't get hurt physically. The Lord will heal me and in time I will be ready for the information she has regarding my fathers whereabouts.

Mom prayed for me and told me how much she loved me. After we talked, I went back to the cell thinking, 'what an amazing Mom I have.' I cried myself to sleep, thanking God for the marvelous things He has done in me.

CHAPTER EIGHT

A Family Meal Please
A buffet of experiences

The next morning I was escorted to the courthouse and was humbled to tears when I saw all of my family, taking up two rows of seats. Sitting there to support me was Mom, Stacey and her son Rustin; Janelle and her two sons, Zach, and Solomon; Ronnie, Clayton, Devin and Sharon. Here they all are in Georgia exhibiting unconditional love for me. Reinforcing the love we have for one another, they truly are Mom's "Amazing Babies," and we are so blessed to have such an "Amazing Mom."

After our phone conversation last night Mom called Stacey, Janelle, Ronnie, and Clayton. She told them what happened to me and they all agreed to fly down here and be in court today to let me know, no matter what the verdict, they love and support me. Devin and Sharon took the day off from their part time jobs to be here for me. They all flew into Atlanta International Airport and took three cabs to the courthouse because there was so many of them.

It turns out the man in the brown pinstriped Dolce and Gabbana suit that had come off the elevator while I was being transported, was the store manager. Here he is at my hearing asking the court to be lenient concerning me. The store is willing to allow me to pay for the items I had stolen if I am willing to sign a declaration I would never return to their establishment. Of course I agreed to sign it. The judge put me on probation for eighteen months and told me very severely, I might add, if I ever darken his courtroom doors for any reason, he was going to put me away and bury the key. I was in agreement with that, I have no intensions of ever going back to jail.

You know, it's difficult to believe, but I can truly say, "I am glad I was arrested" go figure!

After we picked up my belongings from the jail, we went to eat. I shared with my big, loving family about my 'incarcerated revelations.' All of us were crying and the waitress had to bring stacks of napkins to our tables.

When I was done talking, Stacey told us she was deeply scarred also by shame and embarrassment and all during her childhood she took to heart what opinions other people had of her. She told us she was always harassed about having so many sisters and brothers. She shared about her deepest scar as she described it. She was thirteen and had stayed after school to attend a football rally.

There was a young boy by the name of Louis Barnes, he was fifteen, cute, and she had a serious crush on him. He noticed her at the rally and asked if he could sit with her. She being thrilled he asked, told him yes. After the rally, she was headed home and of course he offered to walk with her.

After they climbed down from the bleachers, he walked with her until they were behind the brick wall. She said he pushed her up against the bricks, held her down and told her how he heard her mama had a lot of kids and he just knew she was like her mama and wanted a lot of love from him. She fought him off and ran all the way home crying.

That incident made her resent Mom for having all of us and stamping a label on her. She was so ashamed. She categorized all men as Louis Barnes and thought once a man found out how many kids her Mom had, they would automatically think she was easy. That's when she began wanting to become like Aunt Laura and never have any kids. Stacey was sitting next to Rustin, she grabbed him and gave him a hug and kiss on the forehead and told him he was the best gift God ever gave to her.

Stacy continued telling us she decided to become a therapist, specializing in children's needs because of the level of shame and embarrassment she had experienced as a child.

Being the oldest of seven children, when she was young she felt it was her "duty" to make people not feel uncomfortable about her coming from a large family. She told us after she began to spend quality time in the presence of the Lord; Holy Spirit revealed to her she cared too much about what other people thought of her. She realized a lot of things she did, places she frequented and purchases she made was a direct result of her wanting to impress others.

As Stacey began to trust Holy Spirit more, He healed her of other people's opinions altogether! She hadn't realized it until she received her healing that she was such a people pleaser and after that revelation she began her healing process from the affects of being made ashamed also.

Mom got up and moved to sit next to Stacey and held her in her arms. Again we all reached for the napkins.

Janelle started talking. She explained how like me, she felt so much love at home behind our closed doors. However when she closed the door to leave our apartment, she felt targeted by people who insinuated pity or disgust towards her because of the size of her family. She was very offended by it. She decided to go to school in Detroit, thinking when she left us she would be free from 'the big family stigma.' Being ashamed there was so many of us and resenting the lack we had to endure, when she started Cosmetology School, she told everyone she was an only child.

Janelle wasn't gone a full week before she realized she loved her big family and missed us all terribly. Her classmates would tell stories about their siblings and she realized she was blessed to come from a large family because of all the stories she had to share, but of course she couldn't because we didn't exist!

The first Christmas after Janelle left for college, she just popped up at one a.m. Christmas morning. We were all so happy she was home. Now she is telling us what prompted her visit.

The day before she had attended classes a half day at her school. The remainder of the class time was to be used for their Christmas party. They had pulled names and took turns opening their gifts. When it was her turn to open her gift, she took the wrapping paper off the box and realized it was a picture frame. When she saw the picture of the family with four kids on the box, she immediately thought of all of us. Her heart began to ache. She knew at that moment she could no longer deny having the family she had pretended didn't exist.

That instant, Janelle thought about all of Stacey's dresses, shoes, and coats she had to wait her turn to inherit. She drew the box close to her heart and the tears poured out of her eyes like a faucet. All eyes were on her and she yelled as loud as she could: "**I have three sisters and three brothers, Stacey, Marva, Sharon, Ronnie, Clayton and Devin. And I don't care what you people think about it!**"

She grabbed her things and caught the bus to her rented room and threw some clothes in her suitcase along with the frame and took a cab to the airport, headed to Chicago; home.

Having to fly standby Janelle cried the whole time while sitting in the airport. It seemed everyone there with their families were so happy and that made her heart yearn for hers. Mom asked, "Is that the frame you mailed me on Mother's Day with the picture of all of us on Christmas?" "That's it!" Exclaimed Janelle. Mom gets up and moves to sit next to Janelle now. They hug and we all reach for more napkins.

Janelle tells us after that episode at school, she realized others opinion of her large family no longer had power to influence her. That's when she put her energy into discovering what she was put on this earth to do; and who she was to become. She told us her ability to do hair gives her opportunity every day to minister hope and transformation to those she meets. Janelle is blessed doing what she loves and was born to do, and every time she has the opportunity; she deposits into her sons how loved they are and the fact they have a purpose in life no matter the circumstances that brought them here.

Ronnie clears his throat. Once he had all of our attention, he tells us the large family syndrome had the opposite affect on him. He remembers our home always being filled with love and laughter. He felt lonely when Stacey, Janelle and I left. He said he has difficulty being by himself. He loves to be around a lot of people. He knows he is in love with his girlfriend Camille, but she doesn't want to have any kids.

Ronnie has a four year old son Rodney, by his ex-girlfriend, Monique'. Camille thinks as long as the Addison name will be passed on, there is no need for her to have children. But Ronnie makes good money being a Longshoreman and wants a house full of kids.

He told us whenever anyone comments about his mama having so many kids; he always comes back at them with, "Do you see how fine my mama is?" He has always thought having three older sisters gave him an advantage over his friends because he had an automatic revolving door to meeting girls. Growing up he has always known he was blessed to have a warm, loving Mom, because all through his childhood, his friends wished their mothers were like his.

And his father Herman was and is always there whenever he's needed. Ronnie said he never saw us defined as "too many children." He thought it was cool. His sisters were all fine like his mother, even his baby sister. He turns and gives Sharon a wink. Mom and Sharon both got up and sat Ronnie between the two of them and gave him a double hug. We all said at the same time "Ahh," and had a group laugh.

Clayton says, "My turn." We all stop laughing and turned our heads to look at him. His voice is so deep, and even though his skin tone is light, his facial features are just like Herman's, he looks just like his father did when we were little except Clayton is five shades lighter than his Dad.

Clayton works with Herman at the delivery service, and makes good money for his age. He spoke also, about the fun he remembers having when we were all home. He looks at me and says he is glad we are having a reunion here, in ATL. Ha, ha!

He says listening to us; today he realizes he loves his girlfriend, Belinda. The mother of his two sons Clay Von, almost four years old and Clyde, just turned two. He wants a lot more kids so they can experience the love, nurturing and fun he had growing up. He also had a revelation, Belinda has been telling him he has a fear of being alone, and now he realizes she's right, he does not like it when there's no noise.

The reason being; we grew up with a lot of it! When Clayton gets back to Chicago, we are gong to have our family's first wedding. He is going to marry Belinda, and not just be the father Herman has taught him to be. But the husband Belinda deserves, he is going to start taking his family to church and get his relationship back right with the Lord. Mom got up, walked over to Clayton and told him she was so very proud of him and gave him a hug and sat next to him.

We all turned our attention towards Devin. He started with, "Ditto, big Bro. I hate being alone also. I get very uncomfortable in small settings. Listening to all of you today, I realize that I also miss the old days when you were all home. And what you said about worrying about what other people think, I'm going to look pass what my friends think and 'Man Up'.

I'll be eighteen, and I am so passionate about carpentry like my father. Marva thanks; your going to jail has made me take a deep look inside of myself also. And I love you for that. In fact, I love all y'all." He reaches for a napkin. You know it; Mom is on the move again! And we are all reaching for more napkins.

And Sharon, poor baby she told us she suffers from loneliness. Can you imagine that, the baby of seven and she suffers with loneliness! She also remembers when the house was full of life and laughter.

Mom moved Sharon, Devin, Clayton and Ronnie to Oak Park when Sharon turned twelve and sharon doesn't remember the tough times we often talk about. She loves it when we all come home for special occasions. The love we share for one another and the diversity in our lives is exciting to her.

Sharon dreams of having a large family also so she can love and nurture her children like Mom does us. She told us she wants to become a school teacher and teach first and second graders. Sharon asked us all to be in prayer for her. She wants to hear clearly the instructions of the Lord. So she can please Him and be blessed in her obedience. We were all blinking back tears as we took turns hugging her and each of us told her we were proud of her and will always love our "baby sister."

Mom was the last to hug Sharon and told her she would support her in whatever the Lord has for her to do, but please, please wait and get married to a good godly man before having that large family, please!

Finally, Mom had the last say. After we all sat down she started by thanking God for her parents, Freeman and Loretta Montgomery and how they loved her, her baby brother Jason and her big sister Laura. She used the same pattern her parents used raising them, to raise us. The only difference was our fathers were not living in the home with us.

The Lord had blessed her with men who had good hearts. Men who would see her and her kids in need and regardless who fathered them, they would be a means of provision for us and she was very thankful for that. Mom told us she often wondered when she was younger, had Sterling lived, would he have fathered all of us.

The older she became, she realized the plans of the Lord are often not like our plans. One of her favorite scriptures happens to be Proverbs 19:21 which states: ***"There are many plans in a man's heart, Nevertheless the LORD'S counsel-that will stand."*** Mom accepted that and sought after His plans and not her own. The day she accepted the Lords plans for her life, she no longer lived in shame, fear or regret.

Mom told us she was not exempt from the remarks people made about how many children she had and the number of different fathers. Whenever people were bold enough to ask her why she had so many kids, she would tell them, "My kids and I share a lot of love. I pity people that don't have a lot of love because they tend to have a lot of judgment instead." That line was always followed by silence.

Mom cleared her throat and became really serious and said, "Each of you need to always remember the Lord has a specific assignment for you, and you were born for that purpose. There is a path that only you can tread and that path is limitless. You are to consult the Lord and not other people as to what your assignment is and remember, He will always confirm His Word. Listen to me with your hearts. You need to understand your childhood was only a chapter in your lives, not the whole book. You truly are my 'amazing babies' and together or separately, you will do great things for the Lord. I love you and I am oh so proud of each one of you.

Marva's being put in jail may have began as disapproving, yet encouragement and good has come out of it today." Mom is starting to tear up now. "I want you to know that I love you, you amazing babies!" When she finished talking, we were all crying. We all hugged and took a minute to look one another in the eyes and express how much we loved each other.

After our meal and reunion as Clayton put it, we all took cabs to the parking lot where my car was and they followed me to my house. Mr. Williams had the chance to meet all of my family and he even had Sharon look through a few boxes to find his old camera and took pictures of all of us with him.

I took my family by groups to the airport. It was seven-twenty p.m. as I drove home from my last run and I couldn't stop thanking the Lord for what He had done for me and my family. Later they all called to let me know they made it home and each one shared with me about how our meal together ended up being very cleansing.

Mom was the last person I spoke with. She gave me information on my father, the name of his law firm and a phone number. I was a little surprised to feel a slight twinge of anger when she brought up his name, but I decided I need to confront this matter head on.

The fact that I had a father who did not love nor wanted me, had a direct link to my writing bad checks so I was determined not to let procrastination have its course in this matter.

CHAPTER NINE

Finally We Meet
Extensions of My Life

I never could have imagined, even with my imagination, any good resulting from me going to jail, but it turned out to be the gateway to my abundant life. My life before jail, as I knew it was minute compared to now.

I went to work Tuesday morning and decided before I phone Malcolm Harris I would look up his firm in our office index first. The information Mom gave me was astonishing because it so happened, the firm I worked for listed Harris and Jones Law Firm, LLC as a Chicago reference regarding any corporate law matters and Harris and Jones was second on the list, which means they were highly recommended.

My boss Samuel; "Sammie" Swartz, knew Malcolm Harris personally. I shared with Sammie that Malcolm Harris could possibly be the father I had never met. Sammie phoned Chicago, spoke with Malcolm Harris and arranged a meeting for us here in Mableton, Georgia.

After I caught up with my staff about Monday's work, I went back into Sammie's office and this time I closed the door and sat down in front of him. I told him the reason I was absent yesterday was I had been incarcerated for theft and had written personal checks with intent to fraud. I told Sammie I would totally understand him requesting my resignation and would not harbor any hostility because I was wrong.

Sammie listened attentively then stood up, pushed his chair in, walked around his desk with his eyes fixed firmly on the carpet. He walked over to me and put his hand on my shoulder. I was sitting down watching every move he made, as his hand touched my shoulder I looked up at him bracing myself; thinking he was going to tell me to pack my belongings and get out.

As our eyes met he said, "Marva, we all have made mistakes we wish we hadn't. Your being honest with me is indication of your repentance. Even though you are young, you happen to be one of the finest accountants this firm has. Keep up the outstanding work you're doing, and you'll be just fine."

After I thanked him I said I needed to cut back my hours so I could attend church regularly. He told me to leave early anytime I need to. He wondered why I worked such long hours. Most supervisors put in six hours tops and call it a day. The firm is very fortunate to have me with my skills and will accommodate me in any way necessary. I left Sammie's office knowing what the favor of God looked like!

Later during my lunch I had Kayla and Lisa meet with me in the department head's conference room and I sat down with them and explained how I had been incarcerated for writing bad personal checks and it was a direct effect from me not keeping my relationship with the Lord constant. I explained to them I need to spend less time focusing on my job and I would prefer to meet with them every other Friday for dinner since now I would be getting off work earlier.

They told me they understood and really only waited for me to get off work to spend time with me. After we left the conference room I felt like I was the Lord's favorite child; He truly loves me!

That Wednesday after I was released from jail, I phoned Pastor Houston's Ministry. The prison ministry is an extension of their church and a full time counseling staff is provided. When I phoned for my appointment, they took my mailing address and mailed me a questionnaire to complete and return to the office in order to provide the counselors assigned to me background information before I was seen. My appointment was scheduled for the following Thursday and the session was very informative.

There were two counselors assigned to me a Mrs. Reed and Mr. Henderson. When I arrived, they asked some questions, took a few notes and they each rendered their recommendation.

They recommended I find a church close to my home and job. Also that I cut my working hours back because my job was so demanding, it shifted my focus off the Lord. My distraction led me into the 'religious trap mode' which the enemy loves because then it becomes easier to totally disconnect from a relationship with the Lord all together. They both told me I need to build more on relationships, both horizontally as well as vertically.

Because I was introduced to revelation of the Word at an early age, and the call on my life, I must be planted in a revelation Word based assembly. "*For everyone to whom much is given, from him much will be required; and to whom much has been committed, of him they will ask the more.*" Luke 12:48b.

They told me my spirit man must be fed and kept balanced for me to obtain and stay the path set for me. Then the counselors explained how commonplace it was for people that are from large families to believe they have relationship skills perfected. However most, not all people from large families tend to cling to the familiar. They suggested I join a book club or some bi- monthly social event to work on my relationship skills with people other than family and co-workers.

Also, they suggested I seek the Lord for my assignment; my job was not what I was born to do for the kingdom. I agreed with all that was said. I signed their "Recommendation Agreement Form." They said it would be kept in my file for five years which is the State of Georgia's required time for the ministry to keep archived. At that time my records will be destroyed. They assured me all information acquired was kept confidential. After they closed the session with prayer Mr. Henderson informed me my name would remain on their thirty day prayer of agreement list.

I was given a packet with a list of suggested churches, and some pamphlets with scriptures to read in times of trouble, and phone numbers that provided additional prayer lines.

I took their advice and after visiting three of the churches on the list they gave me, on the second Sunday in September, I joined Christian Fellowship Ministries with presiding Pastor Wilbur Gordon and

First Lady Gwendolyn. Christian Fellowship Ministries is located between my home and job.

Exactly two weeks to the day I was released from jail, Malcolm Harris flew into Atlanta, GA. We met at the exclusive, private, for membership only, "Ample View" Country Club and restaurant located downtown Atlanta on the top floor of the Weber Stock building. It is top notch with ambiance like you've never beheld. The food is to die for and everything served on a plate melts in your mouth. Sammie arranged for us to use his membership as his guest.

I was not nervous at all to meet my father; I think I was still a little angry that he would write a check and poof! Expect me to be gone. Even though I had forgiven him, I wanted him to see how well I turned out without him in my life. Not to be mean or anything but so he wouldn't feel guilty. I figured he probably felt bad enough not knowing what happened to Mom and his baby and I really wanted the Lord to get the glory for how well I turned out. My father told me later he was nervous about meeting me because he didn't know what my mother had told me about him.

He is a very good looking man for someone who will be turning fifty-two in March. Even with his beautiful wavy salt and pepper hair, I could tell he was extremely handsome as a young man. He is six feet two and very dark, with perfect pearl white teeth. His oval shaped dark brown eyes are deep set with real thick eye brows and lashes.

His chin is almost a perfect square shape and the skin on his face is so clear, as if he has never had to shave and he keeps himself physically fit. Tonight, he is dressed to the max with an Armani three piece silk blend navy suit. His shirt is a pale and dark blue pin striped topped with a modest pale blue and soft gold tie.

When the elevator door opened, I stepped into the lavish foyer and walked around the enormous live tropical flower arrangement sitting atop an antique mahogany round table and came in full view of my father. I stopped in the middle of the room with my mouth opened. I was wearing my silk blend navy Donna Karan pant suit with a pale blue blouse and a soft gold scarf around my neck. We were dressed alike down to our navy shoes.

He was standing at the hostess counter and when he saw me standing there, his eyebrows raised and his jaw dropped. That moment was very moving for me. I was thinking, 'so, this is Malcolm Harris, my father, the man who stopped time for Mom.' He eyed me up and down and said, "Hello Marva." I stood there watching how he looked at me. I knew his thoughts. I look just like my Mom. She's five foot two and I am five foot five. Whenever I go home to Chicago, people are always calling me Cynthia until they come close and realize it's me.

Every ounce of love I had for my father surfaced at that moment. I dashed into his chest, fighting back tears. I said, "Finally we meet." He put his arms around me and hugged me so tight, all the doubt of him not loving me vanished and I knew he loved me as much as I loved him.

The hostess told us we could be seated now. We ended our embrace. He grabbed my hand, bent over and picked up a dark brown leather bag. I used my free hand to pat under my eyes drying the tears that had fallen being careful not to wipe off my makeup.

The hostess took us to a table by a window with a view of the city and she seated each one of us at opposite ends of the table. As I sat down and settled myself, I looked up to see Malcolm Harris; my father staring intently at me. He asked me to please excuse him for staring it's just that I resembled Cynthia so much. I looked like he remembered her twenty five years ago.

He asked how was she, had she ever married, did she have any more children. I answered his questions real short. He said he was sorry for asking about my mother when we were here to get acquainted with each other. While our eyes were locked on each others; I slightly nodded my head yes and said in a low voice, "very perceptive."

I started talking. "When I was seventeen Mom told me the story of how you two met. She also told me about the night you wrote her a check after she informed you of my forthcoming arrival. I was angry at her for waiting so long to tell me the truth about you." He leans into the table while his eyes pierce mine and says, "Marva, I need to tell you how remorseful I am for not being there for your mother during her pregnancy and being absent in your development. As it turns out, you are my only daughter. I have a measure of love for you I can not begin to describe. Please, I beg your forgiveness."

He extended his hand over the table towards me, my intention was to glance at his hand but when I did, Mom's words to me that day at the Laundromat replayed: "...this dark manicured hand..," I sat there staring at his hand and started crying. He stood up, turned, grabbed his chair and sat it down right next to mine. He sat down and put his arm around me and pulled me to himself. Then he positioned himself at the end of his chair and began patting my back like I was a baby being burped.

All I could think of was, 'this is what he would have done when I was a baby' and I mean I lost it!

I covered my face with my hands and I commenced to sobbing. He stood up and pulled my chair out and around to face him and I felt his cheek on my head. Now he's stroking the back of my head. I pulled away from him and looked up into his watery eyes, and said, "Daddy!" His voice broke as he said, "Yes, baby." I stood up and we clung to each other, both of us sniffling. We let go of each other and both say at the same time, "I love you." We chuckle at the same time as we each reach for a napkin on the table.

Just then the waiter comes. As we wipe the tears from our eyes, we listen to tonight's specials. As soon as the waiter walked away from us, my "Dad," moved his place setting right next to mine. He told me how blessed he was to finally get the opportunity to meet me and he was so glad he was saved and how comforting it was to him; knowing the Lord as a healer.

He told me he had been healed of a lot of hurt, most of which he brought on himself. He had wonderful experiences of the Lords healing power, but the one hurt he was never able to be completely healed of was me.

Twenty four years earlier, he had gone to a meeting with a client one afternoon near our old neighborhood and he stopped in a Drug Store to purchase some mints and so happened to run into Ms. Turner; our neighbor where Mom lived when they met. He asked her about Mom, she told him Mom had a baby girl April nineteenth. He asked Ms. Turner if she knew where Mom moved.

Ms. Turner told him all she had was a phone number and she could not breach Mom's trust by giving it to him since she knew we had moved to be rid of him. He told her he respected her loyalty to their friendship and he gave her his business card and wrote his personal phone number on it and asked to have Mom please get in contact with him. To his dismay, Mom never called.

He described to me how he would walk down the streets of Chicago, and wonder if when he saw a little girl that might be my age, if he had seen his daughter. Tears started to stream down my face when he told me that. He put his hand on top of mine. He told me if I wanted him to stop talking about this subject, he would; he did not want to hurt me in any way. I told him I had the same fantasy about him since I was seventeen.

He looked into my eyes and tears began streaming down his face. He gently squeezed my hand, wiped his eyes and softly said, "You may look like your mother but you definitely have my persona." I smiled and told him I could see why Mom fell in love with him.

He told me he really loved my mother and was scared when she told him she was pregnant. He never did get back with his wife. When he realized he loved Mom and had made a dumb mistake, it was too late.

My Dad explained to me how he was in his first year of college when his ex-wife became pregnant with Malcolm Jr. and because he was raised to do the right thing, he married her. He was always busy juggling school, his job and helping when he could with each new arrival. After the practice was stable he finally had a chance to sit still long enough to realize he was not in a happy marriage.

Being in practice exposed him to a lot of divorce cases and he witnessed first hand many instances where the children suffered more than the parents. So he was weighing which would damage his sons less; growing up in a loveless home or a divorced home; so he separated to sort things out.

When he met Mom it only took him two days after watching her interact with Stacey and Janelle for him to know he was in love with her. She was so loving and gentle with them. She never hollered or cursed them, he knew she was a loving, nurturing woman and he was head over heels in love. He filed for divorce two weeks after they met and was waiting for absolution.

When Mom told him she was pregnant with me, he freaked completely out. He imagined getting married all over again because he had to, he was so scared he lied. As soon as he closed the door behind himself, leaving her that night he knew he had made a mistake. He loved my mother so much but now he had made himself a coward and a liar.

So, he would stand on the corner and watch her, trying to figure out how he would approach her and tell her he wanted to make a life with her and not his ex wife. He knew he had hurt her and was trying to figure out how he could redeem himself. He went to the apartment several times and put his hand on the door to knock but he didn't think she would believe him. So he kept watching her from the corner. The check he had written to her was never cashed and she didn't look pregnant. He had no idea what if anything she had done about me.

After she moved away, he ran traces on her and came up empty, so he thrust himself into his business hoping his past would just disappear, but he kept wondering how she and the girls were doing. He ended up drinking heavily and the whole responsibility of running the business was left on Jones and Jones suggested he check himself into a clinic and that's what made him realize he needed a Savior.

That's when his life changed for the better. Holy Spirit began healing him emotionally and revealed understanding to him, which he said he very much needed. Again, he asked me to forgive him for being fearful and foolish and could I allow us to get to know each other. I told him yes.

While we ate he told me about the "Harris family calling," and his personal experience being born again. His face lit up as he explained how blessed he is now walking in obedience to the Word of God and living the abundant life. His grandparents on both sides were saved and practiced walking in the spirit and raised both his parents to seek after the Lord with their whole heart.

His parents met in church and raised all of the "Harris tribe" as they were called, to live life according to the Word of the Most High God and experience life and not just existing.

After we ate, he put the dark brown leather bag on the table and took out pictures of my brothers and their families. He told me about each one of them.

Malcolm Jr., thirty two, married to Pilar for eight years. They have six kids, four boys, Malcolm the third, Keaton, Avery and Myles. Two girls, Mallory and Samone. They are both entertainment attorneys.

Next is Thurston, almost thirty one, and married to Megan. They have three children all boys Thurston Jr., Teague and Terrence. Thurston is CEO to one of Chicago's leading computer software companies. Megan owns three Day Care Centers in downtown Chicago.

Then there is Norman, twenty nine, married to Lacy for two years. They have a son, just a little over a year old, Norman Junior. Norman and Lacy own a very lucrative marketing firm also in Chicago. Just this morning Norman phoned him informing they think they are pregnant again, she has to go to the doctor to confirm.

My baby brother, Mason, just turned twenty seven. He has been married for six years to Chyane. They have twin sons, Brice and Sebastian. All of my sister-in-laws are very beautiful.

All of my brothers look like their mother Juanita. The only attribute they have of our Dad is his height. As he put the pictures away, he asked me if Mom was married. Before we left, I gave him her number.

Dad called me the next day and informed me he had arrived back to Chicago safely. He told me my Harris side of the family wants me to get to know them and he wanted my address for my grandparents. They were not computer literate and wanted to mail me pictures of him when he was young. That was the ice breaker for me and them. I kept repeating to myself over and over, "I have grandparents!" Dad told me to buckle up; there was a lot of Harris', a lot of love and inquiries coming my way.

The next day Dad phoned and asked me to tell him about myself. I told him about my being incarcerated and the jailhouse revelation that prompted me to find him. He listened very intently and when I asked if he had any fatherly advice, he said we all make mistakes when we are young, we are supposed to learn from the experience and not keep repeating the same mistake. He said he was very proud of me, I could have a drug addiction, several babies without a husband, live in prison, or even possess a mean bitter personality, and he was so thankful the Lord kept His Hand on me.

Then he gave me the Harris chronicle, his mother and father, Pearl and Garrison, who are in their eighties and still living in North Chicago. Their union brought Uncle Jonathan, Uncle Benson, Aunt Camille, Uncle Wesley, him and Uncle Hershel.

My Aunt Camille died at the age of thirty nine to breast cancer. She never married nor did she have any children. Dad said the family still has a hard time with their only daughter and sister's death, especially during holidays and her birthday in October.

My grandparents mailed me pictures of Dad and my aunt and uncles, along with talking to them for hours over the phone. Their six children has given them twenty-eight grandkids and I am the only female grandchild they have and they are very excited I am a part of them. Nana Pearl told me Uncle Jonathan has seven sons. Uncle Benson has five sons, Uncle Wesley has five sons, Uncle Hershel has six sons and Dad has four sons and me.

She told me almost word for word the conversation she had with my Dad the day he phoned to inform her and my grandfather he found out he had a daughter and how he was so confused when I was born. She asked me to try and understand how terrified he was at the dilemma he had put himself into.

Nana Pearl said, and I quote, "I do not believe in speaking ill of anyone dear, however, Juanita was a gold digger, and an evil, spiteful one at that, and that's all I have to say about that one!" And Nana wasn't kidding, she changed the subject and has never brought up Juanitas' name since. Nana Pearl loves her grandsons with all her heart; however, she is thrilled to finally have a granddaughter she can spoil rotten.

Learning about my father's family and knowing Mom's family history I can see why family is so important to the both of them. Aunt Laura is five years older than Mom and she is more like Mom's mother than her sister. You see, Mom's mother, father and brother, Jason, were all killed in a tragic auto accident, during a severe Chicago snow storm.

They were driving Uncle Jason to a nearby hospital he was only nine years old at the time. He had a very high temperature and the ambulance service told them it could take hours before someone would be able to give them an estimated time of possible arrival, so my grandparents took the chance of driving him.

Mom was twelve and Aunt Laura was seventeen and engaged to a Melvin Pearson. After my grandparents died, Aunt Laura was forced to raise Mom, Mr. Pearson disappeared and that made Aunt Laura full of resentment. When Mom found out she was pregnant with Stacey, she was glad to be in the position of being on her own with State Assistance, so Aunt Laura could finally go on with her life. After they buried Sterling, Mom moved in with the Townsend's until her assistance came through and Aunt Laura sold the house, moved and left no forwarding address.

It wasn't until after Ronnie was born Mom received a phone call from Aunt Laura, asking for forgiveness. Mom invited her over for Sunday dinner and as she was leaving Aunt Laura said; "I don't think I can get used to kid's noises." So, she never visited us again, she keeps in touch by mail and phone and she has never married.

Knowing how both my parents had to bury someone they loved at an early age. I really understand why they each appreciate family and make so much emphasis on how important family is.

Well the following Saturday Clayton and Belinda set their wedding date for February ninth. They are going to have a small ceremony at the office of the Justice of The Peace and have a wedding reception at their apartment afterwards. Stacey wants us all to chip in as a family and give them money as a wedding gift so they can put it towards closing cost. She feels our gift might motivate them to purchase a house; they surely qualify for some first time buyers programs.

When I told Sammie I wanted to go to Chicago in February for my brothers wedding, he said he would check with one of his judge associates about getting my probation amended to include permission for me to go to Chicago and attend the wedding. That's when I had planned to meet all of my Harris family. I was so looking forward to it, I could hardly wait!

However, two days after I met my Dad, Mom phoned to tell me she had heard from him. I called home the very next evening, and my Dad answered the phone. I thought I had dialed his number by mistake. He told me I had dialed Mom's number and he was there to pick her up, they were going out to dinner, on a date! I almost dropped my phone. Mom and Malcolm dating! I couldn't believe it. After that dinner date; they became an item.

They attend church together and Dad takes the four of them to Sunday brunches afterwards. Stacey, Ronnie, Clayton, Devin, Sharon and even little Rustin; has told me how much they like my father. They tell me how happy Mom seems to be, and how it seems she's never been that happy before. Janelle said she can hardly wait until Clayton's wedding so she can meet him, she can hear Mom smiling through the phone when they talk and she knows it's because of my Dad being in her life now.

I was experiencing excitement like never before from both sides of my family. I had a big family before I met my Dad, now my family is enormous!

I changed my office hours to eight-thirty a.m. until five p.m. so I could attend church regularly. Talk about perfect timing, I needed the extra three hours to talk on the phone with my new extended family.

After I joined Christian Fellowship Ministries I attended the mandatory five week new member's classes. The classes are held Sunday mornings during the time allotted for Sunday School. Once we complete our new member's class, each of us is assigned to our Sunday School class according to our age group.

The second New Members Class I attended, some of us in the class agreed to have lunch together after service at a nearby café. As it turned out, most of us are close in age group and we had a good time talking about the things we have in common living holy. A few of the class members are married and have small children. I think there were maybe five of us that were single and a few of them shared about how they felt ready to get married and start a family.

The following Sunday after service we went to eat and while we were waiting to be seated this new guy in our class, Anthony "Tony" Russell, introduced himself to me. While we were being seated at the table, he made an effort to sit next to me. He told me he was born and raised in Stockton California and had moved to Mableton, a month earlier and he works with computers for a living. After talking with him I knew he loves the Lord and is passionate about working with the Youth Ministry.

We hit it off, we talked about the Lord and some of the Bible stories that struck us as interesting during the whole time we ate. The remainder of our new members' classes, he would always end up sitting next to me and sometimes we would talk.

The last day of my new members' class, Tony said to me; "Marva I have two more classes before I'm finished. I really enjoy our conversations and would like to get your phone number so we can continue conversing." I told him, "I enjoyed your company also while we shared class but you should consider taking time to meet other members in the congregation, you might find that you enjoy conversing with them also. See you around." And I left the room.

The next Sunday, right after Sunday School while I was entering the sanctuary, Tony approached me. He said, "Good morning Marva, I want to keep your friendship, I feel comfortable being with you if it's alright, because I do not in any way want to force a friendship with you." He had this look of desperation on his face like he would faint or cry if I said no thanks. So I told him it was ok with me, I just didn't want him to limit himself to only my friendship.

I smiled at him hoping to ease his tension and said, "Tony I think you should take time to meet other members." He stood there as his facial expression changed to strange, and his forehead wrinkled like he was puzzled. I thought to myself; 'what is his trip!' Then I walked around him and entered into the sanctuary. I couldn't figure out why he looked puzzled.

Later that night I talked to Janelle and told her about his reaction. She said, "Girl, don't you know he likes you! Oh wait, I forgot you have had your head in another planet for so long, now you are among the normal. I'll have to let you in on some things." I was shocked, "You think he likes me?" "Ah, yeah, why not Marva you are attractive, single, got it going on. Have you told him how much you make?"

No, we just talk about how good the Lord is. "Well, Lil Sis, keep your head on the ground. Pay attention to his body language, watch him watch you, then you'll know he likes you." I told her okay but I was thinking, 'this is a lot of work, watching to see if he's watching, that's just crazy!'

Wednesday night Bible Study Tony was waiting for me. When I walked into the vestibule he walked up to me and said, "Good evening Miss Marva, I have met everyone in the congregation, and now I would be very honored if you would accompany me into tonight's service." He looked into my eyes as if he were reading them and before I could say anything, he smiled, slightly bent down and extended his arm with his hand on his hip and his elbow pointed upward as if we were about to square dance and said to me; "Let's go get some Word, Miss Montgomery!"

I thought his gesture was cute so I nodded and smiled as I wrapped my arm around his and walked with him into the sanctuary and we sat in service together.

He always says: "The Lord has been nothing but good too me!" As I do, and, in service he is as animated as I am. This man really praises him some Lord. After service he walked me to my car and asked if I wanted to get something to eat. I told him I had plans. He went into his Bible, pulled out a sheet of paper and handed it to me. I took the paper, looked at it, it was his cell phone number. I looked up at him and said, "Oooh, kay!" He smiled said good night and walked away.

On Sunday I entered my Sunday School class and he was standing at the back of my class. He walked up to me and began talking real fast, he says, "Good morning Marva, may I have your phone number since you didn't get the hint to call me?" I told him, "Look, Tony I'm busy!" And started to walk away.

He put his hand on my elbow and I could feel a slight pull; I stopped and looked him in his eyes, slightly lifted my eyebrow and directed my eyes to his hand, then back to his eyes. He let go of my elbow and I said very sternly, "that's better." He says to me, "I'm sorry, I don't ever disrespect women, and I apologize. I really like you and want to get to know you."

I thought about what Janelle told me. I stood there and looked at him, he was standing over me watching my face as if for an answer and I felt as though he was nice, not too talkative so I told him, "Ok, but Tony, you're going to have to slow down, this is all new to me."

A big smile broke out on his face and tenderly he says, "So, can I get your phone number now?" I gave him my home phone number and he asked if we could sit together in service, I said okay. He told me to wait for him in the vestibule after class so we could enjoy service together.

During Praise and Worship service the worship was so intense; we both bowed before the Lord and cried. Pastor Gordon never preached; he allowed the choir to sing songs of worship and the congregation was caught up in worship and a Word from The Lord came forth and edified the whole church. It was so awesome; to spend almost and hour and a half just in the presence of God!

That evening Tony phoned me and apologized again about the elbow and he started talking about the service. We talked for almost an hour on the phone comparing our experiences in worship and expressing how good the Lord was to us. After that he called me every night to say he was just checking on me and we would sit in Sunday School and every Wednesday Night service together.

He really is nice, and he is as sincere as I am about the Lord. We talk about the Bible and our families. He comes from a family of five. Two brothers and two sisters, he is the youngest.

Tony is twenty-seven years old, six feet two; brown skinned and is quite handsome. His eyebrows are so thick and he has deep set light brown eyes and the perfect shaped lips I've ever seen on a man. He keeps his hair cut real close and has side burns that run all the way to the end of his ears and they are always precisely trimmed. I have never seen him in jeans even on Wednesday nights he dresses in slack suits and on Sunday's he is decked down in Stacy Adams, Cooper and Nelson and Sean John suits.

I'm thinking he makes a modest salary. He drives a white Lexus LS460 and says the apartment he leases is only for six months and he has an agent looking for a good bargain on a house. If you ask him anything he looks you directly in the eyes and is precise when he answers your questions which I really like, no unnecessary chatter. He doesn't volunteer any information and he always observes his surroundings.

We seem to have a lot in common. He loves the Lord and we both adore the Lord in our worship. He cries as much as I do. During praise, I dance and leap and he twirls around. The Lord has been good to the both of us and we are not ashamed to say so.

Like me Tony is the only grown child in his family that doesn't have any kids. He grew up in church and spent his childhood fantasizing about life until his parents divorced when he was sixteen. That forced him to enter into the world of reality.

About three weeks after we began talking, I let him have my cell number and we started meeting at the library on Saturdays. We go over our Sunday School lessons together and get so passionate about the lesson; the librarian has to tell us to keep it down.

It has gotten so when we walk into the library, the Librarian gives us the hush finger over her lips; indicating to us to keep the noise down. We look at each other and cover our mouths to keep from laughing out loud.

After we are done with the Sunday School lesson, we read our books for a few hours; he's a reader like I am. Then we go to Lil Lucy's Café, have dinner and we each head home.

CHAPTER TEN

Oh Those Wedding Bells
You won't believe who's falling in love!

I was released from jail August 20th and on October 20th Dad phoned me late, after eleven p.m.. He told me he was going to propose to Mom. I said, "Are you sure, it's only been two months." He laughed and said, "Baby girl, how old are you?" My reply was, "Dad, you know how old..." I couldn't finish my sentence. I thought about him being there at my conception, duh! He says, "And Ms. Marva; I rest my case." He went on to ask if I thought tomorrow would be a good time to ask her and without waiting for my response, he asked me again. He was so nervous, he kept repeating himself.

Dad told me he wants to get married as soon as possible. They are both old enough to go to the Justice of the Peace and commit their lives to each other in the presence of God and witnesses and he wanted all of us kids there. I told him Janelle and I would be in Chicago in February so that would be a good month. Sammie was working on having my probation amended.

Dad told me he had knowledge of some loop holes that would make the probation matter a piece of cake to fix. Then he paused for a moment and said he didn't want to take away from Clayton and Belinda's day. And besides he didn't want to wait until February.

He said for me to talk to Janelle tomorrow and see if next week end would work for her to come to

Chicago. He would provide us both airfare and a suite for the week end if we didn't have anything on our calendars, then he said, "Oh yeah, fax me the court order and I'll fix your probation matter. Baby girl that settles it! I'm going to ask her tomorrow at dinner if she would finally become Mrs. Harris, pray for your Dad okay." I told him I would.

Dad began talking about Mom, he was so excited. He sounded like a young teenager as he talked to me about her. How beautiful she was not just physically but she held an inner beauty that no other woman could ever measure up too. He also told me how she had the ability to make him smile from the inside of his heart out and how his heart skipped a beat when she looked him in the eyes and smiled at him.

Then he said, "You know Baby Girl, the Lord has blessed your mother and I to reunite and I do not want to waste anymore life, on time. I really love Cynthia and want to spend the rest of my life with her." He took on a real serious tone and said, "Baby girl, when a man knows he truly loves a woman, time nor distance can separate that love, those things can only deepen it."

I told him I really was happy for them and would be praying Mom says yes to his proposal. After I finished talking to Dad, I sat and looked at the receiver and it registered; he really does loves her. My father really loves my mother after all these years, wow, go figure!

Without thinking of the time, I hurriedly dialed Janelle. I told her Dad was going to propose to Mom.

She was in shock. She said, "Malcolm is moving a little fast don't you think?" I told her he is about twenty four years overdue. After a short pause Janelle said I was right and she was going to have to juggle some things around to make going to Chicago this weekend happen.

I could hear Janelle smiling through the phone as she told me she was looking forward to going to Chicago to throw some wedding rice on Mom and Malcolm and taking a thousand and one pictures. Janelle became so emotional, she said she couldn't believe Mom was getting married and had rekindled love now after all these years. She started crying and told me Mom deserved to love and be loved and if it could happen to her, it could happen to any of us.

The next day Mom called me while I was at work, on my office phone. I could barely hear what she was saying she was whispering. I had to take her off speaker and ask her to speak up. She said, "Malcolm is acting strange. Marva, he just phoned me here at home and asked if I were home. Then he asked if I wanted to go to dinner tonight, I told him yes and he asked me again. He started to stutter saying, "You sure, uh, uh, you sure, you want to go to dinner tonight, uh you want to go to dinner tonight uh you sure?

Marva I think he's going to ask me to marry him." I asked Mom "Well if he does, what will your answer be." Without hesitation, she said, "Oh girl, my answer is yes. I have never stopped loving that man. Why do you think I never married Herman, he asked me to marry him every week for years?" I replied, "Mom, I thought Herman didn't want to take on the responsibility of financially taking care of all of us." She said, "Ah yeah, and where do you think that thought came from?"

Right then I had a flash back. Mom told me when I was seventeen she loved Malcolm enough to let him go back to his wife, and be happy. I said, "I hope I find a love like yours and Dads, I am so happy for you."

That evening Dad asked Mom to marry him and they called me on Dad's phone with it on speaker while they were at the restaurant. After I said hello all I could hear was the two of them laughing. He said before he could finish his sentence, she blurted out "Yes!" Then he told me to hold on and they said together, "This is your [Mom says] Mom [Dad says] and your Dad," And together as if they had rehearsed they say, "We are getting married and want to invite our daughter to come witness what great and marvelous things God can do. Will you please come witness your parents wedding covenant?" My answer was a loud laughing watering eyes double "Yes, yes!"

The next day two-thirty p.m. my cell phone rings, it was Dad and he had all of Moms kids and my sister-in-laws on a conference call. Him and Mom had all the arrangements made and wanted us to know they were getting married Friday, November ninth, downtown Chicago at the courthouse and we were all going to the Ritz Carlton Hotel Suites on the harbor for the reception. He asked Janelle and me how we wanted our reservations made, did we want to get into Chicago Thursday evening or Friday morning.

We both decided Friday morning would work best and while Mom told us some of the details of the ceremony and reception, Dad made the reservations and came back to the phone and told Janelle and I, we would leave our homes early Friday morning and would leave the hotel together Saturday, close to noon heading back to Atlanta and Detroit. He took our work fax numbers and told us to look for the itinerary within the next thirty minutes.

Janelle has to sponsor a show on that Sunday and had to get back to Detroit, and I could make up for taking off on Friday by working Saturday. We were all excited about Mom getting married and were asking her so many questions and she was happy to answer them all.

I don't know what Sammie and Dad did or how, but the following Wednesday I received a certified letter at work from my probation officer stating I was cleared of my sentence and for me to sign and return the attached document so it could be recorded. Maybe my making the last payment the week before had something to do with it I don't know, but my hand was shaking as I signed and stuffed the document into an over night envelope. As I put the envelope in the "out going" mail stack, I did a little dance step and thought to myself really loud, 'Thank you Jesus!'

The next week I spent getting ready for my trip to Chicago. It seemed to zip by so quickly. Dad took care of all Janelle and my arrangements and when we arrived at our prospective airports, our tickets were waiting. I arrived at O'hare just five minutes before Janelle. We had planned to meet at the baggage and share a cab. As I glanced out at the travelers being picked up at the curb I heard a loud "Tee, Tee Marva!" I turned around to see my two handsome nephews, grinning while running towards me.

While we all hugged, Janelle started crying tears of joy about Mom. She just couldn't believe she was home for Mom's wedding! When we arrived at the hotel Stacey was already there with Dad's secretary, Hillary. They were going over the list they had for the reception, making sure everything was accounted for.

Stacey brought her and Rustin's clothes to the hotel so they could get ready in my room. Before we knew it; it was time to leave for the courthouse. The three of us were so nervous while we waited outside for our cabs when we realized; well, Stacey was the one to bring to our attention, this was like giving Mom away, and even though we were giving her to Malcolm who we all loved we were still giving away our amazing Mom and that's why we were all so nervous. Even knowing why we were nervous, we still cried and hugged each other. Today was the day Mom's last name would be changed.

We arrived at the courthouse early enough to greet the rest of our siblings as they arrived and we all had a moment of "teary eye-dis" as we hugged and greeted one another. I had a chance to see all of my nephews and get some hugs and kisses from them.

My Harris family began to arrive and it was almost strange how they all knew we were waiting for the Montgomery/Harris wedding when they took one look at me. It was absolutely wonderful having all of

Moms "amazing babies," and grand babies at her wedding and the Harris'.

For the first time in my life I saw my mother and father standing together side by side at their wedding. Mom and Dad were both dressed in ivory and I kid you not Mom was glowing! I was so teary eyed and couldn't stop thinking 'I went to jail and look at the good that sprang up out of it.'

My grandparents are here, Nana and Pop, Pop Harris and when I say they couldn't stop hugging and kissing me; I mean just that. I was a kissing sandwich at least a dozen times but I am not complaining I'm really boasting!

Dad is tall like Pop, Pop and dark like Nana. To be in their eighties, they look very good and talk about sharp dressers. They were all decked down, I mean completely 'sparkled out'!

All of my uncles and their wives are here and all of their children and grandchildren, and each one of them took me aside introduced their families to me and welcomed me into the Harris family. All of my aunts and uncles told me my Mom was a sweet and loving woman, and they were so glad to see my Dad finally find happiness.

Uncle Hershel and my Dad can pass for twins. Uncle Hershel has a little less gray hair. When they stand side by side; they look just like identical twins. I was so amazed at that. To see my brothers with their wives and children here, I am almost overwhelmed and Norman and Lacy are expecting another baby in May.

It was literally wall to wall folk in the Judge's chamber, standing room only! The officiator said he's never had a wedding party with such a vast number of attendees to a Friday afternoon ceremony. Sharon counted us and said there were seventy-two of us cramped in that small room to watch Mom and Dad get married.

Dad's secretary, Hillary, coordinated the reception, which by the way was very elegant. His business partner; Cedrick Jones, or CJ; as they all call him, is also here and a lot of their business associates. They all admire Dad so, and speaks very highly of him and of how hard he works.

We took so many pictures and I was surprised to find myself thinking of Tony, missing him actually. I took a few steps back and watched my enormous family interact with one another. Mom's kids interacting with Dad's kids, it was so much love in the room.

In between taking pictures, my sister in laws pulled me aside and encircled me. They told me they loved Mom. She was nothing like Juanita and they were glad of that and, for me to prepare myself because Juanita was spiteful and wanted to see and know all about the love child Malcolm had and the woman that destroyed her marriage. Pilar said, "What she needs to do is look in the mirror for that answer."

They all laughed and seemed to get a great kick out of that. I thanked them for looking out for me and they each told me they had my back. I felt so much love from them, as if I gained four more sisters.

By me getting up at four a.m. to catch my plane, I was tired by nine p.m., so I kissed and hugged everyone and headed upstairs to my room. Mom and Dad had already left at seven p.m. headed to the airport for Hawaii.

I had just pushed the button requesting the elevator to go up to my room, when my cell rang. It was Tony. He said hello and then paused. I thought something had happened so I asked him if everything was alright. He said he found himself thinking of me and he realized he was missing me. Relieved nothing bad had happened, I told him I found myself thinking the same thing.

We are both wondering if its normal for two people, who met less than two months ago should feel like this so soon. Feeling uneasy about our conversation, I told him I was tired and was headed to my room. He said he would talk to me tomorrow and asked what time my flight was due in. I told him I was going straight to work to make up for today and he said "Okay I'll talk to you tomorrow evening, bye." When my phone conversation with Tony ended, I went back into the ball room and told Janelle and Stacey I needed to talk and the three of us went to my room.

Since we talk to each other every day, they know all about how Tony and I study and read together so I shared with them what Tony said to me while I was at the elevator. I didn't tell them how I was missing him; I guess I didn't want to miss him so I denied how I felt. They both told me get to know him a little more; and whatever I do don't believe everything he tells me.

I have never been in a relationship before so I need to take it slow. Discern and trust Holy Spirit to guide me. The instruction they most stressed was for me to consider the fact I make a very lucrative salary and how that alone will draw men like bees to honey. And for that reason alone I had to be cautious when it comes to relationships.

We concluded all I had ever thought about before was church, my education and work. Now that I am having a horizontal relationship and it is with a male not related to me; I need to take one step at a time. I decided to take their advice, after all they have experience with men and they should know. Then we talked about the wedding and reception.

The next morning Janelle and I left together headed to the airport. After we knew where our gates were we had breakfast together and reminisced all that had happened at the wedding and reception. Before we parted we hugged and she told me to; "take Tony slow Marva, you are naïve when it comes to matters of the heart. Be prayerful Lil Sis okay?" I nodded yes to answer her because I was getting teary eyed, not just because we were hugging bye; but because hearing Tony's name sparked some lonely feeling in me.

While on the airplane ride back to Georgia, I reflected on Mom and Dad's wedding, all of us there, the love and feeling of being one enormously happy family. And for the first time in my life, I thought about how many children I might want someday running around in my house.

As a teenager I thought I never wanted any kids. Since I've been on my own, sometimes when I walk the mall and see a happy couple I briefly think about being in love and married some day. But the thought of being married and having children has never entered my imagination. While on the plane I thought three children might be a good number.

Then I remembered what Mom used to tell us, "God is the author of life, no one else." And the day I was released from jail and we were at the restaurant, Mom told us about the plans she had, but the Lord had different plans. Okay Lord, what do you have in Your plans for me!

I deplaned, retrieved my car and drove straight to the office to check on everything. Tony phoned and wanted to meet me for dinner. I told him I was tied up. I really wasn't, I want to put some distance between us, I don't know why, I just do. He said, "How about dessert then." I paused, he asked me if I was alright, did anything happen in Chicago I wanted to talk about, if so he would listen. I said I was just tired and would see him tomorrow at church. He agreed and we ended our conversation.

I didn't do anything at work but think. I have never felt like this before. I like Tony, and honestly; I was scared and wanted to spend some time alone so I could think, you know process what I feel about him and why I feel this way.

Later that evening, Stacey called and asked me if I had heard from Tony. I told her how the earlier conversation with him went. She told me to hang on while she called Janelle. When we were all on the phone, Stacey told me to repeat what I had told her. I did. They both started laughing. "What, may I ask, is so funny?" Together they sang; "Marva's got a love Jones!" Stacey says, "Her very first one." Janelle says, "Yeah Lil Sis, the way the hand of the Lord has always been on you, it may just be the only one."

Stacey's tone turns serious as she says, "Marva you were always different; not in a bad way, just different. Mom would tell Janelle and me that you were born to be a blessing to our family kinda like Joseph. Marva, what was strange to us, was actually very normal to you." Janelle butts in, "Lil Sis; just follow your heart because just like Joseph, the Lord has never led you wrong, even when you were in jail."

Then they took turns telling me how they felt the first time they experienced love. I listened, in my heart; I knew they were right; I was scared because for the first time in my life; I was falling in love.

After talking to them I remembered my counselors telling me to work on my horizontal relationships. Now that Tony has carved a little place in my heart, I find myself wanting to resist him which is what my counselors advised me against doing. I need to really work at this...

The next day I met Tony in the church parking lot, he was there waiting for me. He asked if I was okay. I told him I was. He says while wrinkling his forehead, "Marva, why are you lying to me?" I was shocked he actually called me on my lie. He gently put his hands on my shoulders, looked me in my eyes and said, "Girl, I'm in love with you. I know your heart beat, it beats like mine." Did he just say he's in love with me?

My heart was beating so fast and when I began talking I heard my words come out of my mouth as fast as my heart rate. I said, "Tony I'm afraid. I have never been in love before." Then I felt my eyes get real big because, I didn't know whose voice was coming out of my mouth. The voice I heard was trembling!

I felt tears forming in my eyes and I started talking real fast so I could get my words out before tears took over. "You are the first male I have ever spent more than two hours with that is not related to me." I stomp my foot and say really loud, "I'm afraid to open my heart and allow you full access." I stood there wide eyed and mouth opened; staring at him in wonderment.

He removed his hands from my shoulders and took both my hands and clutched them in his while looking me in the eyes and said very calmly, "Fear is an emotion, emotions can be conquered, and I know that from personal experience. Marva Montgomery I will always protect you and you will never have to be afraid of me; okay."

He smiled and raised his eyebrows as if he were waiting for an answer. I shake my head yes and smile back at him and let out a sigh of relief. He put out his square dance elbow and said, "Alright now, let's go get us some Word Miss Montgomery." I slipped my arm in his as we walked into the church together.

Tony and I went to lunch after church and we talked. He told me he had a serious crush on a young lady when he was in the twelfth grade, but he had never been in love until now with me. I told him I had never even looked at boys when I was younger. I kept my head in the church until I went to college and then all of my attention was placed on my education and keeping my grade point up.

After college I put all my attention on my job and now he has come into my life and I need to figure out how to be in a relationship, and it really is a shame a class on relationship is not offered in college as a course.

He said he wanted more than a relationship, I was what he wanted in a wife, the woman he wanted to teach and train his children, all ten of them. I reacted loudly, WHAT! He laughed and told me he wanted to see my reaction to his number. How many the Lord gives will be okay with him, he really didn't have a number and he just wants a healthy, happy family.

I sat looking at him. I was so scared. He doesn't even know me. Oh no! I can't tell him about my going to jail, no; that's none of his business. How can I slow this down? I say to him, "Tony let's just take it one day at a time, OKAY?" He put his glass of water down real slow as he gazed into my eyes and says, "I won't rush you, I give you my word, I'll wait."

As soon as he said the word "wait" I realized I had been holding my breath while he responded to my request. Then my heart began to race as I thought, 'what would I do if he had said he wouldn't wait?' Now I know I love him, and don't want to lose him. My goodness; this love stuff is work!

We ordered our food and talked about the sermon until we left. All that week, we talked on the phone about our opinions on marriage and children. By the end of the week I wasn't afraid any longer in regards to marriage and children. I was afraid of telling him about what I had done to be incarcerated.

And how in the world was I going to tell him I made more money than he did!

CHAPTER ELEVEN

Layover From the Honeymoon
Time to come clean!

Saturday morning Mom and Dad phoned me from Hawaii. They planned to stop in Mableton on their way home tomorrow. They have a three hour layover and want to take me to dinner. I was so happy they were coming to visit me. When Tony phoned, I told him I was going to dinner with my parents after church tomorrow, and how excited I was. He asked if he could tag along.

I felt like he was hurt he had to ask so I apologized to him and said I should have invited him. He said, "You see Marva, we have the same heart beat. Girl, I love you." I closed my eyes and took in a deep breath and softly said, "Tony, I love you too!" A loud "YES!" was his reply. I opened my eyes and the biggest smile appeared on my face. After a moments silence, he sounded real serious and asked me to meet him for lunch before we go to the library. Since he was so serious I agreed to meet him.

While we ate he talked about his brothers and sisters and I listened carefully wondering when he would talk about what made him get so serious over the phone but his conversation was light. As we stood up to leave the restaurant Tony told me he needed to get his car washed and offered to treat mine to a wash if I would go with him. I thought, 'good I'll tell him at the car wash about my being incarcerated.' So I told him, "Sure, my car could use a washing." And I followed him to the car wash.

We went inside and sat down while we waited on our cars. I was trying to figure out when to tell him about my weekend in jail and I was looking for a nice relaxed moment. I noticed Tony was acting fidgety and kept looking at me. When I would stare at him, waiting for an opening to talk, he would start flapping his car wash ticket around and shaking his leg as if he was nervous.

My stomach was in knots and I kept going over and over in my head, 'okay, say Tony, I have something I need to tell you.' But every time I started to say it; he didn't seem relaxed enough or maybe it was me not relaxed enough, I don't know.

Anyway, I almost blurted out: "I have something to tell you." When the young woman announced his car was ready. He jumped up so fast I began to wonder what he was so afraid of. Surely he didn't sense I had something bad to tell him. As I grabbed my purse and stood up my car was announced, whew! Saved by the announcement!

Neither one of us said anything, I just followed him to the library and rehearsed my speech all the way. I'm going to tell him today and get this over with.

We found a table inside the library and pulled out our Sunday School lesson. After he pray I placed my hand on his and told him I had something to tell him. He looked surprised and sat back in his chair and said, "Ok shoot." I took in a deep breath and looked him in the eyes and told him about my writing bad checks and all about how I was arrested and my weekend in jail. While telling him about what happened to me when I felt embarrassed, he put his hand on mine and gave it a gentle squeeze.

I explained to him how my boss, Sammie and my Dad, a corporate attorney, had to get my probation reversed so I could attend my parents wedding. When I finished telling him, I was both relieved and scared he wouldn't want anything else to do with me. I slowly lowered my eyes down to the table waiting to hear his response.

He said very tenderly to me, "Marva, baby look at me." I took in a deep breath and swallowed real hard as I looked up directly into his eyes; he was smiling and said, "I know that was very difficult for you. I love you even more for your honesty, and I didn't think I could possibly love you any more than I already did."

As tears began to fill my eyes I looked at his facial features and thought, 'wow! Love really does cover a multitude of faults.' I smiled at him being relieved as I blinked back tears.

We went over the lesson and really got into it. It was about faith without works; coming from James 2:17-26 which says: ***"Thus also faith by itself, if it does not have works, is dead. But someone will say, 'You have faith, and I have works.' Show me your faith without your works, and I will show you my faith by my works. You believe that there is one God. You do well. Even the demons believe- and tremble! But do you want to know, O foolish man, that faith without works is dead? Was not Abraham our father justified by works when he offered Isaac his son on the alter?***

Do you see that faith was working together with his works, and by works faith was made perfect? And the scripture was fulfilled which says, 'Abraham believed God, and it was accounted to him for righteousness.' And he was called the friend of God. You see then that a man is justified by works, and not by faith only. Likewise, was not Rahab the harlot also justified by works when she received the messengers and sent them out another way? For as the body without the spirit is dead, so faith without works is dead also."

We had such a good discussion the librarian had to come over to our table and tell us to shush; and I do believe when she turned around to leave she rolled her eyes at us!

After we completed the lesson we pulled out our books and I pretended to read. I kept thinking, 'I can see myself married to Tony, yeah.' But every time I tried to imagine us getting married I couldn't see anything. So I closed my eyes and silently prayed, "Lord, why can't I see myself married to Tony?" Right then I saw my check register. Instantly I opened my eyes!

My heart was pounding so fast and I was breathing so hard! How can I tell him how much money I make, he is so confident, so, so, macho. He is not the kind of man that is going to like the idea of his wife making more money than he does. I have to figure out a way to tell him how much money I make.

I was a nervous wreck. I couldn't read or think about anything except, 'how is he going to react? I have never seen him go off, as a matter of fact, I've never seen him mad and I really don't want to see it happen today. I have already told him about my writing bad checks and going to jail, now to add this; he might think it a wee bit too much.'

When we closed our books to leave Tony asked if I was hungry because he wasn't. I didn't want to go to Lil Lucy's Café either; my stomach was in knots. All I wanted to do was think of a way to ease my salary into a conversation. So I told him I wasn't hungry just tired.

We left the library agreeing to see each other in the morning at church. Good, I don't want to talk on the phone, I am so wound up.

All that evening I practiced how to approach Tony. I paced the floor, looked in the mirror and rehearsed what and how I was going to tell him. Keeping my salary from him was eating me up inside. In an odd way I felt as though I was lying to Tony and it made me feel sneaky and conniving. I wrestled until after midnight, finally I thought, 'Marva, if you don't tell him tomorrow, you will burst, so tell him after your parents leave, just tell him.' Then I was able to rest and fall asleep.

After Sunday School I felt I had enough faith to tell Tony and he would be able to handle the fact his wife will make more money than he does. I was settled and calm. Why did Pastor Gordon preach on Ephesians 4:24 – 27, which states: ***"and that you put on the new man which was created according to God, in true righteousness and holiness. Therefore, putting away lying, 'Let each one of*** *you speak truth with his neighbor,' for we are members of one another. 'Be angry, and do not sin'. Do not let the sun go down on your wrath, nor give place to the devil."*

Pastor Gordon broke down the different ways of lying including omission. I believe I squirmed in my seat the whole time he spoke on omission thinking about how I kept my salary from Tony. Finally I told myself, 'you're okay. You'll tell him today as soon as Mom and Dad leaves. You're okay with this one, just relax, you got this.'

After service I rode with Tony to the airport and noticed he was acting nervous. He kept adjusting the air controls and turning the radio volume up and down. I didn't know if he was nervous because it was my first time riding in his car or because he was going to meet my Mom and Dad. I told him not to be nervous my parents were good people. That didn't seem to calm him, so I let it go. He'll find out for himself when he meets them.

When we pulled up Mom and Dad were standing outside at the curb in front of the baggage claim. I didn't tell them I would not be driving, they both know my car so I rolled down the passenger window and stuck my head out. Dad saw me, waved, smiled and told Mom, "Babe, here she is over here." Dad stepped up to my window and gave me a kiss on my cheek and said, "Love you baby girl," and stepped over to the rear door and opened it for Mom while Tony and I both turned around to face the back seat.

Mom steps into the car and leans towards me and kisses me on my cheek and says, "Hello amazing baby," then looks at Tony and says, "Hello." While sitting down. As Tony and I watch her he says hello and I say hello amazing Mom.

When Dad sat down he had his eyes fixed on the door and after he was sure it was closed he looked up over towards Tony and he took on the strangest serious look. His forehead wrinkled and he squinted his eyes as his neck slightly jerked back. He said "Well, hello." Quickly looks at me and smiles. I knew something was wrong. He started talking about the weather here being different from what they had just left, then Mom started in.

When we arrived at the restaurant all of us were standing at valet parking. Tony extended his hand out to Dad. When Dad extended his hand to Tony, Tony grabbed and pulled Dad close to himself and said something in his ear. I watched as Dad shook his head yes, and quickly glanced towards me and said, "Marva ask your Mom about the pineapple she almost bought; we're right behind you." I knew he meant for us to walk ahead of them so I turned to see Mom's reaction. She had already started walking towards me and when she was standing next to me I asked, "Did you see that, what do you suppose that was about?" She says, "Don't worry, we will soon find out."

Mom and I walked inside the restaurant and waited at the hostess counter for them. I watched the both of them as they walked towards us. They both seemed comfortable with each other as they were talking and walking. Tony stopped and turned towards Dad. Dad stopped and turned towards Tony. They don't seem upset, but I was wondering what the grab and hug was about, but like Mom said, we'll soon find out, here they come.

While we ate, Mom and Dad were telling us all about Hawaii. She pulled out some beautiful pictures of Hawaii and the Hotel they lodged. They were only in a few of the pictures and Dad commented on how they spent most of the time in their honeymoon suite. Mom playfully hit him, blushed and said, "Malcolm, not in front of the kids!" I was moved seeing them so happy and in love.

When we were all in the car headed back to the airport, Mom said to Tony, "Forgive us for doing all of the talking, please tell us about yourself." Dad blurted, "Cynthia baby, let's not scare the young man off." And he started talking about the cost of living in Hawaii. I turned around and looked at Mom, she raised her eyebrows and hunched her shoulders. I turned back around and played along. I knew Dad was nervous, I just didn't know what about.

We arrived at the airport early for their flight home. Dad said, "Tony just pull up curbside, we can say our so longs right here." Tony did as directed and when he pulled up to the curb he put the car in park while we all stepped out of the car. I hugged Mom and she turned around and hugged Tony. When Dad hugged me, he had this serious look on his face.

I was almost frightened. He pulled me close and asked me in my ear, "Baby Girl do you love Tony?" He let me go and looked into my eyes while waiting for my answer. I told him very slowly, "I think so why?" He quickly glanced towards Tony, looks back at me directly in my eyes and says in a real stern voice, "Make sure and don't have any doubts, okay?" Ok, I answered. Now I'm really confused.

As Tony drove us to my car, I watched him. He was relaxed now, quiet, but relaxed. I'm the one nervous. We said our goodnights, and he watched me pull off before he left. I was so uneasy I thought this love stuff is entirely too much work, what just happened!

Tony didn't call me and I thought about calling him but I didn't know exactly what to say to him, after all it was Dad who set off these alarms in my head. I tossed and turned all night, first because of how Dad acted, then because with all the strange acting I forgot to tell Tony about my salary.

Every time I closed my eyes all I could see was my father's face when he saw Tony in the car and how Tony grabbed him, then Dad's expression when he told me to be sure I loved Tony. Then my imagination kicked in.

Was Tony a hit man? Why was my father so serious, was he afraid of Tony. Dad is an attorney maybe he knew Tony from a criminal case. The suspense was eating at me. I hardly slept at all thinking about the look on Dad's face. By the time my alarm clock went off, I had Tony wanted by the FBI.

I decided to call in sick today I was too tired to go in. After I called the office and left my message I laid on my chaise and fell asleep until nine-thirty a.m.. I called Dad's phone and as soon as I heard him say "Well hello Marva." I say to him, "I caught the look on your face when you saw Tony, what's going on?" He laughed and said he told Mom that I probably wouldn't get any sleep and would phone them this morning. He says, "Now there's no doubt; you are definitely a chip right off my block." He told Mom I was on the phone and for me to hold on. He was putting me on speaker so she could hear this.

My father told me he recognized Tony from the internet. Tony saw his reaction and figured since he was a corporate attorney he might have heard of him. Dad said he promised to give Tony the opportunity to tell me himself but I was his baby and blood is thicker than mud. Tony will just have to understand. By this time I am almost to stroke out! "Yeah, yeah, what is it? Is he a serial killer or what?"

Mom burst out laughing. Dad says, "Baby girl, he is one of the wealthiest computer magnates in the world. And he loves you dearly!" I had to wait for my heart to slow down. It was beating so fast from the suspense. It took me a moment then it registered what Dad said.

Now I'm mad. "He lied to me!" Mom spoke right up. "Marva, have you told him what you do for a living?" Almost yelling and with an attitude I reply, "Yes I have!" Dad asked, did you tell him how much you make?" I went silent. Mom says, "Then you can understand why Tony has been private about his income. Baby, you two are so much alike." Mom and Dad both are laughing. I am stunned. Dad tells me to go on the internet and look up Russell Brothers' Computers. And to call tomorrow and let them know what happens. As they hang up all I hear is the two of them laughing.

I went on the internet and pulled up Russell Brother's Computers and there was a link that led me to Robert Anthony Russell's bio. I could not believe what I read. He was wealthy! Tony is actually wealthy.

His father was in some type of computer business with his uncles in Northern California. Tony went to college and came up with the first computer game of its kind ever invented.

As it turned out, the Russell Brothers tried to find a backer for the games invention. Because they were African American, they were turned down before anyone knew exactly what they were selling. Tony went overseas with his father and found an open door for his families business. That was three years ago and the bio was last updated six months ago.

While I printed the bio I phoned Tony and when he answered, "Marva you're not at work?" I told him, "Look, meet me at Lil Lucy's Café in thirty minutes!" And I slammed the phone down, talk about heated!

All the while I was driving I thought about how I was tormented trying to think of how to tell this man how much money I made and here he is wealthy! He told me he worked with computers, yeah like it was a common job and after my upset stomachs and sleepless night I find out this man is wealthy! Wealthy! Go figure, not rich but wealthy!

When I pulled up in front of Lil Lucy's he was standing near the front door waiting for me. As soon as I stepped out of my car and slammed the door, he took one look at me and started to apologize. "Marva I'm sorry. Your Dad told you didn't he? I knew I should have told you yesterday on the way to the airport. I tried to tell you Saturday while we ate and again at the car wash. Baby I tossed and turned all night last night trying to figure out how to tell you today."

Now I'm three feet from him and he throws both hands up as if I'm the police and says, "Ok Marva, I'm sorry, but, the women that just come after me for my money, Marva, baby, please let me explain." He looks as if he's about to tear up and while shaking his head "NO" he says in a real low voice, "I don't want to lose you over money." By now I am standing in front of him.

I say to him, "You, Robert Anthony Russell pursued me remember!" I'm pushing on his chest with my index finger and continue talking, "And money is not a problem with me." He's shaking his head yes, now he's hunching his shoulders. I tell him how much money I make a year.

He smiles, grabs me and hugs me real tight and before I knew it, he had picked me up off the ground and was twirling me around. He puts my feet back on the ground, bends down and kisses me in my mouth! I have never been kissed by a boy before, and to be kissed for the first time like this! My goodness, I'm standing here looking at him as he has his eyes closed. I'm thinking, 'Oh yeah I know I'm in love now!'

He opens his eyes and stands straight up and we both stand gazing at each other as if we are seeing each other for the very first time. He asks, "Did you feel that?" I shake my head yes. He says, "That's what I call confirmation! Will you marry me Marva?" I replied, "Yeah." I could barely speak I was actually weak in the knees.

Tony says, "Marva I love you girl, I love you!" He stood eyes wide and a smile to match, then he put his square dance elbow out and while I stand staring at him I slide my arm in his and we walk into the café. My knees were still shaking from the kiss.

After we sat down in a booth he apologized for not telling me who he was, and explains to me how people change when they find out he has some money. I told him I understood because I was struggling myself with how to inform him about how much I made. We both got a kick out of that and began laughing. He asks if there was anything else we need to put on the table, if so let's do it now. We would laugh and shake our head as if in unbelief every time we looked at each other.

Tony turned serious and took my hand and said, "Marva that kiss was so electrifying the next time we kiss will have to be after we say I do. I don't want to be tempted not to wait for our honeymoon. I want us to be obedient so the blessing will be on our marriage. After we eat let's go to the church and sign up for classes and get married the day after our last class. How do you feel about all that?" I agreed.

While we were eating I shared with Tony how I had come to this place in my life because I went to jail. My experience in jail was a life changing one, for my good actually. Going to jail was the fork in the road of my life. The end of shame ruling me and the beginning of me walking into my abundant life. I was headed down a path that would have made me miss all of the abundance stored up just for me.

I fought back tears as I told him I had only become a member of Christian Fellowship Ministries two weeks before he did. I continued telling him that it was less than thirty days I had repented and turned all the way around and restored my relationship back with the Lord, less than a month before we met!

It was truly amazing how God had orchestrated our meeting and I was at awe how the Lord's plans required me to get back in fellowship with Him so I would walk in the Word and produce a prosperous, healthy soul, capable of handling the wealth He wants to entrust me with. The Lord truly does work in mysterious ways and...yes, He has been nothing but good too me!

Before we left the Café to sign up for our premarital classes at the church, Tony told me how thankful he was we were so compatible when it comes to the Kingdom of God. He looked me in the eyes so lovingly and said, "Marva you truly are my good thing and if the Lord had sent me around the world to find you I would have gone. I love you so much." As tears formed in my eyes I replied, "Tony I love you too."

EPILOUGE

We left Lil Lucy's café and went straight to the church and signed up for the premarital class. Pastor Gordon interviews couples interested in premarital classes and refers them to one of the Ministers on staff. However when he interviewed us he decided to do the counseling himself.

Pastor Gordon enlightened us to the procedures when joining the church. First is the mandatory five weeks New Members Class and three months after the new member has settled in, Pastor Gordon has a one on one meeting with the new member to determine where they fit in the ministry.

In our case, Pastor saw the calling on Tony and confirmed the Youth Ministry Anointing and also confirmed my teaching anointing. So we decided to have the wedding here in Mableton since we will settle here. Our wedding is scheduled for Saturday, December ninth, right after our last premarital class Tuesday, December fifth.

Before we left Lil Lucy's Café, the day he proposed, we phoned our parents and told them we were engaged. That Thursday evening his father and three uncles flew into one of Atlanta's private airports to meet me. Tony picked me up from work and we went to his Dad's suite.

Tonys' uncle Henry asked Tony how we met and Tony said the church he attended all his life had a lot of young attractive ladies but, while he was growing up no one noticed him. As soon as the news of the family's fortune hit the papers, he couldn't get a moments peace. He dated several of the young ladies and was very disappointed to find they had different moral values than he did.

After two years of dating women and finding himself still lonely, he realized he was tired of being single and asked the Lord to guide him in selecting a wife that had the same affections for the Kingdom of God he has. He was lead to go on a three day fast.

While on the fast he read the book of Genesis and was so impressed by chapter twenty-four. He couldn't get the story of how the Holy Spirit joined Isaac and Rebecca out of his mind. After the fast he decided to go to the land of his father to find his wife. He knew his grandmother Russell's first name was Mable and her mothers name was Georgina. He went online and brought up the map of Georgia. Then he looked to see if there was a city with the name of Mable in the state and up popped Mableton.

His father says, are you for real? Tony says, "True story" and he looks at me and continues. "When I landed in Mableton, I asked Holy Spirit to lead me to the church my wife to be attended. I visited two churches, the second church I attended, after being ushered to my seat, I glanced around the sanctuary and there was Marva worshipping the Lord with all her heart. One look at her and I knew she was the one.

I joined the church and when she came to New Members Class, I knew the Lord had sent both of us here to meet. I asked the Lord to let me be completely sure she was the one, when I struck up a conversation with her, let her be the one to bring up anything concerning the book of Genesis.

A group of us went to a restaurant and I sat next to her and the first thing to come out of her mouth was, "we are so blessed to be the seed of Abraham." There was no doubt, I knew I was blessed to find her." Tony had me tearing up. This was the first time he told me that story. I felt blessed to have been found by him.

His father had sparkling grape juice sent up to the suite for us to celebrate. After the toast to our engagement, room service delivered dinner for us to break bread together as a symbol of their approval of the future Mrs. Tony Russell. While we ate, each of Tony's uncles and his father told me something about how Tony was as a child. They are all nice people and very serious about their relationship with the Lord. We all spent the remainder of the evening getting to know each other.

Saturday morning Tony had us flown to Detroit so he could meet Janelle, Zach and Solomon. We took them to a restaurant and before we left Janelle told me how proud of me she was. Watching the blessings that followed me facing my fears head on had inspired her to start looking for her father, James Lott. She asked both of us to include her in our prayers.

On the way back to Mableton, we stopped over in Chicago and ended up spending the night with Mom and Dad. Tony met all of my family including the Harris side. Pop, Pop told Tony that I barely had enough time to become a Harris and here he comes wanting to make me a Russell. Nana said she thought it was pretty amusing how she couldn't get a grand daughter without getting another grandson. They hugged Tony and said there was plenty love to include him.

All of my enormous family love them some Tony and I saw how he interacted with my nephews and nieces, I could see the Youth Ministry all over him, and he truly has a passion for the youth.

The following Monday Tony's mother, Stephanie flew out. We had dinner with her in her hotel suite and she told me about how much of a loner Tony was growing up. He played video games all the time and she was amazed at how he still kept his grades up. She wanted him to play sports like his brothers but he had absolutely no interest in anything that had to do with outdoors. He was just born different from the other boys and it took her a while, but she accepts the fact Tony is supposed to be different.

Stephanie said she and Winston divorced eleven years ago and they still can't have a civil conversation without arguing, but she promised our wedding day will not have any of their drama. She would be on her best behavior for her baby's wedding. She is really nice.

That evening when Tony took me home, we sat in his car and he told me everything he went through when his mother and father divorced. He said he never want his children to ever experience the pain associated with severing a family.

He was so hurt emotionally he started smoking weed, running the streets with a bad crowd and became promiscuous. After several months of being rebellious, he grew tired of not having fellowship with the one constant person in his life; the Lord. He repented and started counseling sessions with the Youth Pastor at his church. Tony realized acting crazy was his way of handling being divorced from the life he once knew when his mother and father were together. Holy Spirit really ministered and healed him and his worship went to a higher level after that.

After Tony dropped me off I entered my Condo, and began to leap and give thanks and praise unto the Lord for my childhood and for Him healing my emotional scars and the shame attached to it. Mom never gave us a father that lived in our home, but she sure gave us a Father that lived in our hearts.

Tony took me to lunch the following Saturday just outside of Mableton to a place I never knew existed; the Wynn Gate Botanical Resort and Hotel, it is magnificent. We took a tour of the grounds and decided it was perfect for our wedding. It has one hundred and eighty hotel rooms, and the wedding chapel has a wall of windows that display the grounds and it makes the best backdrop ever. Tony will rent the resort for the weekend of the wedding for all of our families to stay.

I am at awe of the wonderful works God has done in my life, and when I think that I went to jail, jail and all of these blessings resulted from my being obedient. I cant' help but say aloud; "Lord, you have been nothing but good too me! Thank you!

SHAME IN ME

SUMMARY

Most parents are not aware of their child's introduction to shame, embarrassment, humiliation or low esteem. Let's understand; life includes negative and positive. We cannot shield anyone from life's lessons. Our job as parents is to teach and train our children how to handle life and the lessons it is sure to bring. The sooner we notice the inception of their exposures, the sooner we can work on cultivating their understanding and confidence. Let's take a look at this fictitious character as she encounters her life's experiences.

First Grade: Marva, only in the first grade and even though she doesn't understand it she has been familiarized with "public and personal depreciation." She looked forward to getting her sisters shoes. In her innocence, she thought everyone who noticed her noticed and admired her shoes. After Marvas' classmates made fun of her, she experienced humiliation and now the "trust" in her own opinion has diminished.

From now on, she will second guess what she likes, and she will wonder if it will be "acceptable" to others. She needs to be educated on how everyone has a built in "opinion [view] thermometer" and as long as her opinion is not self centered or harmful, she is entitled to her own preference.

As Marva gets older, she may change her view even then, the change should be by choice and not imposed. She should be encouraged and reinforced on how much her opinion matters and that her opinion is important, whether she voices it or not. Even if her opinion is not popular, she still has a right to her opinion.

This reinforcement is necessary to combat low esteem. Sometimes in large families, there will be a few children who are not confident in their own opinion because they admire the opinion of the more vocal sibling. They tend to think that particular sibling is better capable of expressing themselves. If there is anything to be said, they think that sibling should become the spokesperson. This is acceptable, only if the opinion is shared. There should not be any fear of speaking ones opinion.

Third Grade: Now Marva is aware by personal experience, of how other people look down on large families. At home her mother is teaching her and her siblings to be close, proud of each other and to love one another. Marva is now assembling her world at home with the world outside.

She is associating if and how she will impact her world. It is important she understands life has disadvantages that sometimes are unpleasant, but we gain knowledge from them. Now, Marva understands from experience the consequences of living with lack. Again, it should be stressed to her that it is her "worth" that will determine her outcome in life, not someone else's opinion of her.

She needs to know that lack is only temporary and learn the principle of saving. Lack only becomes a life style when your mind is set on lack being a constant in your future. Now would be a good time to teach her how to set goals. Save for a certain purchase. Live within the means you have now, but reach for better.

By now shame is trying to become embedded in her, and not just an emotion she'll experience. Should shame get rooted, it will carve out the course for her life, and shame never carves out anything pretty. Obviously, in the story she ended up in jail.

Right now, because of what Marva has been exposed to, someone needs to give her constant reinforcement and support in focusing on the beauty of who she is and what she can become. This will establish the significance of balance to her life. So she will understand she may have lack in her life now, but her future has great things in store for her not only will she appreciate no more lack but her purpose in this life that no one else can fulfill.

Jr. High: Now she is understanding life's reproduction. She thinks her mother is oblivious to the hardship in the home. To her, all her mom sees is her "Amazing Babies." She is prejudiced by the lack in her home, by her math, there would be more to go around, if there were less of them. She is embarrassed at not having money to do what she thinks is minimal for everyone else because they don't have large families.

Embarrassment caused by the fact there are different fathers, only intensifies her resentment. At this stage in her life, she has added up everything she has been taught. Her view of life is determined by the bad choices people around her have made. Now she will start saying things like, "I will never have any kids." Or, "I am only going to have one child."

These comments are indications of her interpretations of the cause of lack. It's not too late to direct her on the positive path. Marva needs to make her focal point on the fact God is the author of life, and there is purpose and destiny for each one of her mothers children.

Marvas' energy should be directed toward the life of people who made/make a difference in this world, and her local surroundings. She should become aware of the potential placed in her and concentrate on her preparation to cultivate it. She needs to know and understand; "the significance of one" and how awesome it is, especially when the hand of the Most High God is upon them!

High School: The time to link reality with all of the information collected through one's life. Perhaps Marva has chosen to leave her home state in hopes of living where no one knows her family history. She has no idea when she packs her belongings her "shame" will be leaving along with her. Now she has added illegitimacy to her source of shame.

Anger and hurt will only impair her having a healthy rest of her life. She must examine, and remedy her anger and hurt and forgive before she will make choices that will produce contempt in her life. What she needs to do is talk to her mother and find her father. Not to cause them guilt or shame, but for her to get an understanding and healing.

Let's take a look at the word shame. The Bible defines shame as "disgraced, to wound, taunt or insult." The dictionary states shame as "a painful feeling caused by exposure of unworthy or indecent circumstances or conduct." We all have built in mechanisms to protect ourselves, physically and emotionally. The emotional protection we use early in our life becomes a blueprint for us to use throughout our lives.

Our introduction to disgrace, insult or shame causes us to question ourselves: "what did I do?" That way we won't put ourselves in that position again. Or perhaps we think: "okay, they got me that time, but I won't let that happen to me again." Right away our inner mechanism goes to work on protecting us. The more we are exposed to insult or shame, we continue to look for what will protect us until we find what works for us.

For instance one child may hit the person causing them to feel pain from insult or shame. Another child might cry and yet another child might do something funny to counter the pain. In the story, Marva refused to let her attacker know she was in pain. We will find some way to protect ourselves.

As we mature in our walk with the Lord, we realize the protection mechanism is hindering our praise and worship. The pain associated with shame causes us to ask ourselves, "What will people think when they see me praise and worship my Lord? Will I feel ashamed?" or, "What will the Holy Spirit make me do? When I yield to Him will I look stupid?"

If my life's quest has been to impress others, when it's time to praise and worship my Lord; that mechanism will automatically kick in. It will assume the position of protecting me from becoming ashamed of how I will look. Proverbs 4:23 tells us ***Keep your*** *heart with all diligence; For out of it spring the issues of life.*" The issues here are the emotions entwined in our hearts.

We praise to invoke the presence of the Most High and set the atmosphere for worship. The more we know Him, the more we can be like Him. When we have emotions like shame and low esteem, we must appraise those emotions, to enter into pure worship.

Like in the story, we don't always know what is holding us back from entering completely into the presence of the Lord. If we don't examine ourselves we will just stay where we are and not grow and develop spiritually; and may even dwindle away. That's why so many start out on fire for the Lord and so few stay on fire.

Marva had a very strong relationship with the Lord until it was time to go to the next level spiritually. Not willing to probe her soul, she ended up backing off completely. Some people continue to attend services, give first fruit tithes and offerings but never prosper; just stay in the same position as far as spiritual growth goes. This produces a form of godliness. [2 Timothy 3:5]

We must always remember we grow spiritually and naturally. Think of growing spiritually as developing in school, passing from one grade to another. Growing spiritually is very similar except, we perfect our soul which is our emotions, the way we think, our personality, who we really are; the soul actually gets perfected according to the Word. We bare the fruit of the Word. The reason I'm going into such detail is because shame disables a lot of us and introduced early in our lives without a proper understanding, becomes a principality that will rule every area of our future.

In this story we see how shame entered by way of a large family and being illegitimate. Shame can enter the heart other ways also. Growing up in an alcoholic home or with someone physically or mentally handicapped, even with a visible imperfection or a family secret are also ways shame can find entrance.

Using Marva as an example; as an adult, she is very likely to store up food or purchase a lot of clothes, and absolutely must have the most expensive furniture and automobiles. Just to have and keep an image. She believes she has to prove she can afford all of these things now and not go without, like she had to as a child. Money constantly flows through her hands; however, the constant fear of being without is the fuel that motivates her purchases.

Because her motive is not healthy, she will never become satisfied. There is always a bigger, better, improved, whatever out there. Her decisions will be made according to how it looks, rather than if there is a need or investment. Making a purchase to prove to a nasty sales person you can afford it. Or how about borrowing money to put gas in the car to get to work because, are you ready for this one; we bought a pair of shoes to impress a co-worker.

Yeah, doesn't that sound ridiculous? Yet it's done everyday. When the same mistake occurs repeatedly, and the sorrow deepens, and becomes so intense, in our finances or relationships, it's time to get some "Word counseling".

What opinion do you have of yourself? What is your motive before you go shopping, or before you pursue a new relationship? Be honest, that is the only way deliverance is obtained.

You have the heart of a pleaser, a server. Because shame was introduced to you at an early age, and took root, the pattern of your life was cut out according to someone else's image of you. Your process of thinking must be reversed; the Lords opinion of you must be the only opinion that matters to you now. The way to delete the opinion of others and reconstruct your thinking pattern is to study the Word.

Romans 12: 2, Amplified Version tells us: "***And do not be conformed to this world [any longer with its superficial values and customs], but be transformed and progressively changed [as you mature spiritually] by the renewing of your mind [focusing on godly values and ethical attitudes], so that you may prove [for yourselves] what the will of God is, that which is good and acceptable and perfect [in His plan and purpose for you]***."

Matthew 6: 33, tells us if we search for the kingdom of heaven, then the things will come automatically. You need to understand and know when you set your affection on pleasing the Lord; your new pattern for your life will lead you to a place that is good, peaceful, and prosperous. The more you study and get in His presence, the more the Lord's plan for you will be revealed. Overcoming will occur when your mind is renewed, and only by the Word of God. You were created to please God first then He will reveal His plans for you.

In the Old Testament, we see over and over again how after the children of Israel would overtake their enemy, God would instruct them to burn up the enemies belongings. The extreme value of the opinions of others must be consumed by the fire of the Word in your heart.

Holy Spirit will remove the anger and hurt you will feel about how you were manipulated in your thinking. When forgiveness comes; you will realize it was not the people; it was the devil, your enemy that wanted you to walk in error and not live a healthy, vibrant, prosperous life.

The understanding and healing you get will allow you to walk in the direction customized just for you. The Word of God must be the foundation of your new thought process. When you are being drawn to other people's opinion, think on the Word of God. Pull those imaginations down by the weight of the Word.

I can't express the importance of studying the Word enough. It is crucial you get the Word down in you, so every time you doubt, or want to yield to temptation, the Word becomes alive in you. When the Word begins to birth Life in you, the ability NOT to yield to temptation will exist.

Because love conquers fear, a good scripture to think on is Deuteronomy 7: 7 & 8a, *"The Lord did not set his love upon you, because you were more in number than any people, for you were the fewest of all people: but because the Lord loved you..."* Or Jeremiah 29:11 *"for I know the thoughts that I have toward you, saith the Lord, thoughts of peace, and not evil, to give you an expected end."* Write down some scriptures you can meditate on while you are shopping, or before you go on that first date.

My grandmother used to tell me, "You can't worry about what people say about you. What they know, they'll tell, what they don't know, they'll make up."

PEOPLES OPINION IS JUST THAT, AN OPINION!

SHAME IN ME

www.ingramcontent.com/pod-product-compliance
Lightning Source LLC
Chambersburg PA
CBHW070953120726
47910CB00004B/1221